THE TOUGH WINTER

Robert Lawson

When Uncle Analdas, the old, old Rabbit, predicted, "I hold it's goin' to be a tough winter, and needn't nobody bother to deny it," all the Rabbit Hill Animals said he was just getting old and gloomy. But even Uncle Analdas couldn't remember a winter as tough as this. Thanksgiving brought an ice storm and a food shortage, and the Folks went away to bluegrass country for the winter, leaving a neglectful Caretaker and a mean Dog in charge.

All the entertaining animals of the woods and fields of the Connecticut Hill are here again: Little Georgie, filled with bustle and excitement; Father, the perfect Southern gentleman; and Porky, Phewie, Mother, Mole, and all the rest. And this time Willie Fieldmouse, loyal to the Hill to the last, and Uncle Analdas, a hero of the situation, play very important roles in the winter drama.

RL

The Tough Winter

by Robert Lawson

Puffin Books

Blessings on the burrow

of

ALAN and MARY BERRY DEVOE

R.L.

1954

Contents

[7]

The Tough Winter

THERE was a Hill, and on the Hill there was a house known as the Big House. The Folks who lived in the Big House loved and respected all Animals, and the Small Animals who lived on the Hill loved and trusted their Folks— and were not afraid.

So they dwelt there together, the Folks and the Animals, in the greatest amity.

On the Hill there was a statue of the good St. Francis, carved of stone, and holding out his hands in kindly welcome to the Small Animals he so loved. At his feet there was a pool of clear water, and around the pool there was a coping of broad, flat stones. On the stones were carved the words:

THERE IS ENOUGH FOR ALL

Each night there was spread on these stones a feast for the Animals: sweet hay, fresh vegetables, fruits, nuts, seeds, and grain. Each morning the stones were clean.

Being well fed and having decent gratitude and respect, the Animals never so much as set paw in the Folks' garden. Flowers and vegetables bloomed and ripened there all untouched.

Because on this Hill there was kindness, respect for the rights of others, and no fear, there was also happiness and peace.

But peace and happiness do not always flow on endlessly, without interruption, and Folks are not trees, to stay forever rooted in one spot. So it came to pass that. . .

1. Analdas Prophesies

UNCLE ANALDAS, the old, old Rabbit, glared around at his cronies. "I hold it's goin' to be a tough winter," he announced, "and needn't nobody bother to deny it."

The Red Fox, stretched out in the warm autumn sun, yawned lazily. "Nobody's bothering to," he said. "All I asked was how do you know, that's all. How do you know so certain sure?"

"I know all right," Uncle Analdas muttered. "I've ben through more winters than all you young whippersnappers could count on all your claws put together. Yessir, I've ben through regular winters and easy winters and tough winters, and this here winter's goin' to be a tough one, a real tough one, you mark my words."

"I'm marking them," Foxy said and yawned again. "All I asked was how do you *know?*"

"Feel it in my bones, that's how!" Uncle Analdas snorted. "How else would anybody know?"

Phewie the Skunk chuckled. "If you'd put a little fat on those old bones of yours, like Porkey there, you'd wouldn't be feeling things in 'em all the time."

Uncle Analdas glanced at the portly Woodchuck busily stuffing himself on grass and clover. Porkey had far more than a little fat on his bones. His sides bulged, his neck was almost larger than his head, he wheezed and grunted each time he pulled up a tuft of grass, but still he continued to stuff.

"Disgusting," Uncle Analdas said. "Plain disgusting, that's what it is. No wonder folks call 'em Groundhogs. Hey, Porkey," he called, "looks like you're figgerin' on a tough winter too."

Porkey paused a moment, chewing reflectively. "Winter's nothing to me," he answered dully. "Ain't figgerin' on nothing. Easy winter, tough winter — all the same. *I* sleep. Don't see why everybody don't sleep. Best way to pass the winter. All's I'm figgerin' on is sleepin' well fed." He went back to his grazing.

"Fat's getting into his head too," Uncle Analdas muttered.

"Talks stupid-like. Way he is now, any old Dog could take him easy as not. Hope he holes up soon."

Foxy yawned again and rolled over on his back, exposing his creamy underside to the pleasant sun. "He'll hole up when he gets ready," Foxy said lazily, "and no sooner. Porkey never does anything till he gets good and ready. Real set in his ways, Porkey is. Say, isn't that old Bluegrass coming up the hill? Looks like he's in a hurry."

They all turned and watched the approach of Father Rabbit, who did indeed seem to be moving at more than his usual dignified pace. His son, Little Georgie, hopping along beside him, also seemed filled with bustle and excitement.

"Good evening and good luck to you, gentlemen," Father greeted them. "I trust that this glorious afternoon finds you all in good health and spirits?" He paused and sighed deeply. "Much as I dislike to disturb the tranquillity of this pleasant little gathering, certain news has just reached my ears which I feel I must divulge at once. My son, Little Georgie here, whom you all know to be a very observant, intelligent, and trustworthy young Rabbit, has recently overheard a conversation between Tim McGrath, the gardener here on the Hill, and Sulphronia, the cook, which contained tidings of very grave import to all of us. As I was saying, I feel that I must at once divulge —"

"Whyn't you quit gassin' and divulge?" Uncle Analdas interrupted.

"Although this news is important, Analdas," Father said severely, "it is not so pressing as to preclude ordinary politeness. As I was about to say when interrupted, quite rudely I must point out, I — what *was* it I was about to say, Georgie?"

"About the Folks, Father. In the Big House — going away," Little Georgie answered, fairly dancing with impatience.

"Oh yes, the Folks — our kind and generous Folks in the Big House. Well, gentlemen, the distressing fact is that our Folks are departing."

In the stunned silence that followed the Little Animals shook off all their lazy torpor. Even Porkey ceased his stuffing and joined the tense group.

"Going?" Phewie asked incredulously. "For good?"

"No, fortunately not," Father answered. "Merely a winter's sojourn in a more equable climate. As a matter of fact," he went on rather dreamily, "they are departing for Kentucky, my natal state, the land of bluegrass, of fine Horses and beautiful —"

"Never mind the bluegrass and the fine Horses. What about our garbidge?" Phewie demanded.

"And what about our nuts?" the Gray Squirrel piped up. "And the meals they set out for you folks?"

"And the seed for Willie Fieldmouse and the Pheasants," added Porkey, "and the suet and all? And hay and salt for the Red Buck?"

The Red Fox sighed. "It won't be very cheerful of nights with the house all dark and cold and no Folks about. Wouldn't be surprised if I even missed that old Cat!"

"Although the outlook is undoubtedly depressing," Father said, "things may not prove to be as unfortunate as we anticipate. I understand that there will be a Caretaker and his wife left in charge, so there will necessarily be *some* garbage, Phewie, although I cannot, of course, guarantee its quality. As for the rest of us, I feel sure that Folks as kindly and thoughtful as ours have proved to be will not fail to leave orders that we are to be looked out for."

"Leavin' orders is one thing; gettin' 'em done is somethin' else," Uncle Analdas grumbled. "Don't trust no Caretakers, I don't. What I ben tellin' you fellers about a tough winter comin'?" He cackled loudly. "Who's right now?"

[15]

"The situation being as it is," Father went on, "I feel it incumbent on us to adopt the most optimistic attitude possible. In the meantime, though, just to be on the safe side, we had best take time by the forelock and fill our storage rooms to capacity against the uncertainties of the coming winter. I ask all of you to notify your friends and relatives of this approaching change and advise them to store away as much provender as they can manage."

"I got no storage room to speak of excep' my stummick," Phewie complained. "Besides, you can't store garbidge nohow. Don't keep good."

"When're they leavin'?" Porkey inquired.

"Immediately after Thanksgiving, I understand," replied Father.

"Lot we'll have to give thanks fer," muttered Porkey and resumed his foraging with redoubled vigor.

Little Georgie hastened on down the Hill to tell his friend Willie Fieldmouse the news. He himself was not especially worried by the coming departure of the Folks, not nearly as upset as Phewie or Father. He didn't pay much attention to Uncle Analdas; he was always an old gloom anyway.

Of course they would all miss the Folks; they had been so kind and thoughtful. Every evening for the past year and a half they had set out a bountiful meal for the Little Animals. The fields and lawns were lush with rich grain and grass, free for all. There were young fruit and nut trees, just beginning to bear. Around all the property boundaries were NO HUNTING signs. Even invading Dogs were promptly driven off, chiefly by Mr. Muldoon, the Folks' ancient Cat. Old and harmless though he was, Mr. Muldoon could present quite a terrifying front to ignorant wandering Dogs.

Perhaps, Little Georgie thought, perhaps they had gotten a bit spoiled by all this kindness. It might be a good thing if they *were* left on their own for the winter. *He* didn't mind the cold or the snow, if it wasn't too deep. There would always be enough to eat — not much, but enough. A tough winter might be exciting, and there hadn't been much excitement on the Hill lately; things had been *too* easy and peaceful. To tell the truth, he had been just a little bit bored.

Willie Fieldmouse, when Georgie finally found him, felt pretty much the same way. He liked the winter and didn't

care how deep the snow got. For he and all his relatives made their little tunnels under the snow, a great network of tunnels that covered the whole Hill. He tried to tell Little Georgie how much fun it was, how beautiful the light was, coming down through the snow, how easy it was to get food, and how warm and cozy their tunnels were no matter what the weather was outside. It was a great time for visiting Fieldmouse friends and relations too, for they lived in a little world of their own, shut off from most of the other Animals. His special pal Mole would be way down deep in the earth, clear below the frost level. Willie didn't care for it down there; it was damp and stuffy and pitchy-black. Mole wasn't very good company in the winter either.

"But I'll see *you* all the time, Georgie," he promised. "I'll make a special tunnel right to your burrow, just like last year. I don't think it's going to be such a bad winter anyway, just because your Uncle Analdas says so."

"Oh, he's always gloomy," Little Georgie said. "Now he'll have us wasting all this grand weather lugging food home till the storeroom's jammed to the roof with it."

The Mole, who was sunning himself at the mouth of his run, turned his blind face toward them. "You two young 'uns don't know what a real tough winter is," he said. "Ain't had any experience yet. I mind a winter four, five years ago when the frost was in the ground three-foot deep clear to the middle of May. Time I come up top I was nothing but moleskin and bones."

"Sounds just like Uncle Analdas," Little Georgie muttered and continued on down the Hill.

He came across the Gray Squirrel, his wife, and all their young ones frantically gathering nuts and burying them here, there, and everywhere. The Red Squirrels and Chipmunks all scuttled about too, chittering excitedly as they carried nuts in various directions.

"Better hurry up and get to work, Little Georgie," the Gray Squirrel cried. "Goin' to be a tough winter."

"Who says so?" Little Georgie asked impatiently.

"Your Uncle Analdas. Things are going to be bad, with the Folks going away and all."

"Uncle Analdas doesn't know *everything*," Little Georgie said, quite rudely for him. "And if you ever remembered where you buried half of those nuts you'd be better off."

He went off toward the burrow in an unhappy mood, for he knew just how upset Mother Rabbit would be over the news. On the way he passed Tim McGrath, who was also working busily, preparing for the coming winter. He had tied up all the roses and was now building burlap shelters over some of the evergreens.

"Everybody's going crazy," Little Georgie muttered to himself. "You'd think there'd never been a winter before."

2. Harvest Home

MOTHER RABBIT had already heard the news
and of course was having a splendid fit of worrying.
She had set Father and Uncle Analdas to clearing out and
dusting the storeroom, a task they had accepted with rather

ill grace and considerable grumbling. There were eight little baskets set out up near the burrow entrance.

"Now, Georgie," she said briskly as soon as he arrived, "come and get to work for goodness knows there's plenty to do what with a bad winter coming on and the Folks going away and all — and why they want to go away anyway I can't imagine with that lovely comfortable house and Mr. McGrath to shovel the snow and all —"

"The desire for a change, my dear," Father interrupted from the storeroom door, "especially the change they contemplate — namely, to visit Kentucky — is, to me, quite understandable. Unfortunately you have never experienced the beauties of the Bluegrass Region —"

"You and your Bluegrass!" cackled Uncle Analdas. "You'll be glad enough for a tuft of dried-up Connecticut timothy come January or February."

"And, Georgie," Mother went on, "when we go up for our spread this evening I want you to eat well so you'll put on a little flesh for the winter because goodness knows you'll probably need it with nobody to look out for us but a Caretaker — and everybody knows how good-for-nothing Caretakers are if they were any good they wouldn't be Caretakers — and I've gotten out eight baskets — that's two for each of us — and when we've eaten all we want we can bring some home to put away in the storeroom, and tomorrow you and Father and Uncle Analdas can start gathering clover from the South Field and dry it and store it and maybe we'll make out but I don't see how with the Folks going away and all, and why they had to pick this winter of all times I don't see —"

She paused for breath, and Little Georgie went off to admire the sunset.

Later, when the moon rose, they went up the Hill, carrying their little baskets. As always, there was a generous feast spread out on the coping of the pool. The kindly figure of St. Francis smiled down on them; from his outstretched hands clear water dripped with little tinkling splashes. The moon was large and orange, the air misty but warm. Winter seemed far, far away.

At least it did to Little Georgie, but all the other Little Animals seemed to have taken Uncle Analdas's prophecies with great seriousness. Every Animal on the Hill was there, and they all ate most heartily — so heartily, in fact, that there was little left to be carried away. Mother managed to fill both her baskets, and Uncle Analdas one of his, but Father's and Little Georgie's were empty.

"Here, son," said Father, hastily handing his baskets to Little Georgie. "Please take these for me. To think that I, a gentleman from the Bluegrass, should be seen lugging a basket like any old market woman! *So* humiliating!"

They passed Phewie carrying a mouthful of chicken-bones, which he laid down to converse. "Thought I might's well store away a few of these here," he said. "Won't be much nourishment into 'em, but a feller can always chew

on 'em, worst comes to worst. No tellin' what sort of garbidge this here Caretaker and his old woman'll set out,
if any."

The three small basketfuls of food did not make any
great showing on the storeroom shelves, and Little Georgie
sadly realized that he would have to spend most of this
glorious autumn weather helping Father and Uncle Analdas gather clover. He was not very happy about it, for the
fall had always been the season for him to accompany
Father on long rambles all over the countryside. *That* had
been real fun. Exciting too, for they had often been chased
by strange dogs, sometimes even shot at by hunters. But
Father, of course, knew all the tricks and had taught Little
Georgie most of them, so there was seldom any real danger.

Fortunately the Folks increased the size of the nightly
banquets, so there was always enough for all and plenty to
take home. But Mother would not be satisfied until every
inch of the storeroom was filled, so Little Georgie was
forced to help Father and Uncle Analdas cut and dry clover,
tie it in neat bundles and store it away, while the gorgeous
days of autumn slipped by.

The trees strove to outdo each other in brilliant color, the
leaves dried and fell, the nuts ripened and dropped, to be
eagerly gathered by the Squirrels and Chipmunks. Foxy and
the Possums gorged themselves on late-ripening wild grapes.
Porkey, so fat now he could scarcely waddle, lugged arm-
fuls of leaves and hay into his burrow for his winter bed.

Willie Fieldmouse and his cousins ran about day and night, gathering tiny seeds and hiding them in neat little piles all over the Hill.

And still the weather remained balmy. The nights were a bit frosty, but each morning the sun rose redly through the mist, burned away mist and frost, and shone down on the warm brown fields. As Thanksgiving approached with still no sign of winter, the Little Animals began to relax their efforts, and there was considerable jeering at Uncle Analdas and his fears.

"Goodness, Georgie," said Willie Fieldmouse, "here when I ought to be fat and sleek for the winter I'm worn to skin and bone gathering food and hiding it, and probably all for nothing. *I* don't think it's going to be a bad winter. Here's November almost gone and it's still like summer."

"I don't either," Little Georgie agreed. "I think Uncle Analdas is just getting old and full of notions. And here's all the nice fall weather gone and nobody's had any fun at all."

Father Rabbit also protested mildly, but each morning Uncle Analdas would go to the mouth of the burrow, squint up at the warm hazy sky, and pronounce, "Deceitful, that's what it is. Plain deceitful. The deceitful ones is always the worst, and this is the deceitfulest I've seen in years. Wait till December and January — and you'll see who's right."

And so he drove them all to still more effort until shortly before Thanksgiving, when the storeroom was so tightly

[24]

packed that not another twig or bunch of clover could be jammed in. Not content with this, he stowed away a great deal of fodder under his bed, which caused even Mother to protest.

"Never you mind," the old gentleman chuckled. "Come February or March there'll be a plenty of people a-peekin' and a-pokin' under my bed, lookin' for a handout."

Thanksgiving finally arrived. The day was damp and somewhat cold. Low-hanging dark clouds blanketed the sky. Tim McGrath had turned off the water and drained the

pipes leading to the pool, and the figure of St. Francis was tightly swathed in straw and burlap.

In honor of the day the Folks had set out an unusually bountiful spread, but the gathering of Little Animals was somewhat subdued, although they ate heartily enough and packed their baskets solidly. When all had finished Father rose and made a short speech.

"As you are well aware," he said, "our good and kindly Folks are soon to depart for a winter's sojourn in a more salubrious climate. Having had the good fortune to spend my youth in that lovely region, I must say that I view their good fortune with a certain amount of envy. We shall miss them greatly, but since our presence and well-being seem to give them a certain amount of pleasure, I feel we should all demonstrate our gratitude to them by meeting whatever trials the approaching winter may bring with courage and good cheer. That we should preserve ourselves

and our homes to the best of our ability so that we may
greet them in the spring, filled with good health and
happiness."

Going home down the Hill, the Rabbit family overtook
the Red Fox proudly carrying the entire carcass of a turkey.
"How's that for a Thanksgiving haul?" he cried gleefully.
"That'll be something to gnaw on for many a day. And
Phewie's got himself a whole ham bone."

Suddenly Uncle Analdas stopped and held up a paw.
"Here she comes," he announced.

They all became aware that it was snowing, large
feathery flakes dropping silently through the still air. By
the time they reached the burrow the ground was faintly
white.

3. Ice

ALL THROUGH the night it snowed heavily. In the morning Uncle Analdas, always the first up, went to the burrow entrance, butted and kicked his way out through the now deep snow, came back, shook himself well, and climbed into bed again. "A good foot, now," he said gloomily, pulling the blankets up around his chin, "and still a-comin'." In a few minutes he was snoring peacefully.

About noon there was a slight difference in the sound of the softly falling snow, and Father went out to observe.

"Rain," he reported. "A freezing rain. There is a considerable crust on the snow. I had some difficulty in breaking out."

Little Georgie had slept as much as he could and was becoming extremely bored when, late in the afternoon, they were all roused by a sudden commotion at the burrow entrance. In burst Willie Fieldmouse, followed by three of his young cousins. The young cousins, fairly well blown by their tunneling efforts, at once settled themselves by the fireplace. Willie, however, was bursting with excitement.

"Oh, Georgie," he cried, "the old Cat is lost — Mr. Muldoon, you know. The Folks were calling him all night, and the Man has been tramping around the fields all day in this freezing rain and he can't find him. But I know where he is. I found him, but I can't do anything about it."

"You are somewhat overexcited, William," Father said, "and your account lacks coherence. You say the Cat is lost but you have found him. Therefore he cannot be lost. Now suppose you sit down and tell us quietly just what has happened."

"Yessir, I'll try," Willie answered. "Well, we were digging a tunnel to Uncle Sleeper's — he lives down along the wall there, and Mother wanted to be sure he was all right — and suddenly we came on the old Cat holed up under the snow right beside the wall. He must have gotten lost, and when the snow got too deep he just got in a little hole there by the wall and let it snow over him and kept turning around until he had a nice little room all hollowed out. And now he can't get out because there's an awful thick crust on top of the snow."

"The poor old thing!" Mother said. "Isn't he terribly cold, Willie?"

"No, ma'am, I don't think so," replied Willie. "Of course I didn't *feel* him, but it's nice and warm there under the snow. He must be getting real hungry though. That's why we didn't stay around very long."

"The poor Folks!" Mother exclaimed. "And them getting ready to go away and all and the Cat lost and them so fond of him! It does seem to me there ought to be something we could do and him so nice to all of us and never harmed a soul. Oh, Analdas, isn't there *something* you and Father and Georgie could do?"

"Not me," Uncle Analdas answered promptly. "It's agin Nature, that's what it is. Since when have Mice and Rabbits taken to helpin' out Cats? Maybe he ain't ever done nothin' *to* any of us, but he ain't ever done nothin' *fer* any of us neither. Nossir, I ain't one to fly in the face of Nature." He pulled up the blankets and went to sleep again.

"Foxy had a lovely turkey carcass last night," Little Georgie said thoughtfully. "There was a lot of nice meat on it. If we could only get some of that to Mr. Muldoon he'd at least have something to eat, but I guess we can't. Foxy's iced in just like the rest of us."

"I think maybe we can. I know we can," squeaked

[30]

Willie Fieldmouse excitedly. He sat quiet for a time, and they could see him going over in his mind all the maze of Mouse tunnels that covered the Hill. "Look," he finally said, "there's a tunnel from here to our place, and then there's one that goes up through the rock garden to Aunt Minnie's — Father dug that one this morning. Then from there there's a long one up to Uncle Stackpole's, way up near the Pine Wood. I'm sure that's dug by now. Foxy's den is right close to that one, I know exactly where. It'll only take us a little while to dig in to him. Then, if he'll let us have a little turkey meat, we can drag it down and give it to Mr. Muldoon."

"I wonder if he will," Little Georgie said doubtfully. "Foxy doesn't know Mr. Muldoon very well, and I don't think he cares especially about him one way or the other."

"You will have to be most diplomatic and persuasive, William," Father instructed. "Be very polite and use all the powers of eloquence at your command. You might mention that compliance with your request would bring deep pleasure to Mother and me."

"Yessir," replied Willie. "Come on, boys." The three young cousins rose from the fireplace somewhat reluctantly, shook themselves, and scampered up the tunnel.

"It may take some time," Willie called back, "but we'll do our best."

Mother, Father, and Little Georgie sat through the long evening in silence, their minds filled with thoughts of the

[31]

old Cat trapped in his tiny refuge under the icy crust. Mother's thoughts turned mostly to the Folks and their distress. Uncle Analdas snored.

The freezing rain seemed to have stopped, but the wind had risen. Every now and then they could hear the jar and crash of some great ice-coated tree branch falling to earth. Although outside sounds were muffled they could recognize the roar and clatter of trucks plowing the Black Road, could sometimes hear the shouts of linemen battling to repair fallen wires. Finally Little Georgie dozed off.

He was wakened by a cry from Mother and the excited chittering of Fieldmice. There stood Willie and his three cousins, each dragging a long sliver of plump white turkey meat. They were thoroughly exhausted, and Mother insisted that they take a short rest before finishing their journey.

"Well, William," Father congratulated him, "I am delighted to see that your good manners and eloquence prevailed on Foxy. I trust that the mention of my name was also of some assistance."

"He was asleep," Willie said, grinning. "So we didn't

have to eloquent. We had to be awful quiet though —
that's why it took so long."

They resumed their burdens and set off toward Mr. Muldoon's refuge. They were soon back. "He just loved it,"
Willie reported. "He gobbled up every piece as fast as we
could push it in. But we didn't stay around long. He might
still have been a *little* hungry."

Next morning Little Georgie was waked by the voices of
Father and Uncle Analdas. Evidently they had been up
some time, for they had clawed an opening up through the
snow as far as the icy top crust. There they were stopped.
All their pushing and grunting, thumping and kicking,
were to no avail.

"Mebbe the sun'll soften the dingblasted ice," Uncle
Analdas growled. "*Now* who was right about a tough winter, and it hardly begun yet!" He went back to bed.

Little Georgie went out and stared up at the icy sheet that imprisoned them. It looked like frosted glass, with the sun glimmering through it. Apparently the wind was blowing strongly, for he could hear twigs and branches sliding and skittering over the surface. He wished he could tunnel under the snow as skillfully as Willie Fieldmouse, and tried it, but he didn't get very far. Then they had breakfast and waited for Uncle Analdas to wake up.

When he did, an hour or two later, they went out to try again. As Father and Uncle Analdas pushed and grunted the crust *did* seem to be giving slightly. Little Georgie clambered up on their shoulders and heaved and pushed as hard as he could. With a great cracking the ice crust suddenly gave way and Little Georgie was shot out into the blinding sunlight.

He was speechless with surprise at the way the looks of things had changed. Fallen branches, large and small, lay everywhere. Shrubs were flattened. Slender saplings were bent over like croquet wickets. The tall cedars were splayed out like worn-out brushes. And every twig, every boulder, even the red brick house, was sheathed in winking, glittering ice. The wind was bitterly cold, but the sun had begun to loosen the ice, which was now falling from the trees in tinkling showers.

He could see the Man and Tim McGrath attacking the fallen boughs with saws and axes, carefully searching under each one.

[34]

Uncle Analdas shook the snow out of his ears and went off to see if any of the other Animals had managed to break out. Father and Little Georgie hastened along the wall to the spot beyond the little oak tree where Willie Fieldmouse had said Mr. Muldoon was buried. They found the place easily, but though they rapped and scratched no sound came from below the ice. Mr. Muldoon's plight seemed pretty hopeless.

Suddenly Little Georgie had an idea, and without a word to Father he dashed off up the Hill. It was rather tough going, for the icy crust was terribly slippery and the wind was strong. He had a great many slips and tumbles before reaching the shelter of the Pine Wood.

Here the ice had hardly penetrated; the snow was still soft and fluffy. He floundered and hopped through it until he saw the warm brown form of the Red Buck. The Buck had tramped down the snow in a neat circular yard and was quietly browsing on hemlock twigs.

"Good morning, sir, and good luck to you," Little Georgie said politely.

"Good morning, Georgie," replied the Buck, "and how have all you little fellows fared in the storm?"

"Not very well, sir," Georgie answered. "'Most everyone's still iced in, and poor Mr. Muldoon—" He plunged into an account of Mr. Muldoon's plight, ending with a plea for the Buck's assistance.

"Well, I don't know," the Buck answered dubiously.

"Hate to walk in an ice crust—cuts your ankles real nasty. Snow covers up holes and mole runs and stones too—can break a leg easy as not. I've never had much to do with that Cat; ordinarily I wouldn't bother with him. Still and all, we do owe the Folks an awful lot, and I suppose I ought to do what I can to help out. Come ahead, we'll try it anyway."

Going down the Hill, the Buck walked with extreme care, thrusting each hoof gingerly through the icy crust, feeling his footing and withdrawing his hoofs very gently. Little Georgie, in high good spirits, galloped in circles, slithered and skittered and took long breath-taking coasts on the slippery surface. Tim McGrath and the Man stopped their labors to watch quietly as the two Animals passed.

Father had been scratching and thumping at the ice but had made no impression at all, although he thought he had heard Mr. Muldoon mew once or twice.

Now the Buck, rapping on the crust with his chisel-sharp hoof, broke it up and began carefully pawing away the slabs of ice. As he worked closer and closer to the spot where Father thought the mewing had come from, Little Georgie's breath grew short with excitement.

Finally with a gentle heave the Buck pried up one last large slab, revealing Mr. Muldoon neatly curled in his snowy nest. The old Cat rose, somewhat stiffly, shook himself irritably, and without so much as a glance at his rescuers stalked away up the Hill, his dignified pace interrupted now and then by an awkward sprawl on the icy

surface. Father immediately hastened back to the burrow to relieve Mother's mind.

The Man gathered the Cat in his arms and went up to the house, but Tim McGrath continued to stare in open-mouthed wonder. He watched while the Deer, with Little Georgie running gay circles around him, carefully retraced his steps up the Hill. The Buck's ankles were cut and scraped by the crust, and an occasional drop of blood marked his trail.

Tim walked down to the wall; examined the old Cat's refuge, the Deer's footprints, and the pawed away slabs of ice. "Holy Saints," he murmured, "if I hadn't seen it with me own two eyes I wouldn't've believed it! I'm not sure I do now."

He went to the toolhouse, gathered a huge armful of hay, and lugged it up the Hill to the edge of the Pine Wood, where he spread it out beside the Deer's trail. "Feedin' the wild stock!" He laughed at himself a bit sheepishly. "I must be gettin' soft in the head. Next thing I'll take to readin' books."

4. City Folks

NEXT morning Little Georgie was the first one out and about. Sliding and coasting on the icy crust yesterday had been grand fun, and he wanted more of it. Uncle Analdas wasn't interested in sliding, and of course it was far beneath Father's dignity.

Most of the other Animals were still iced in, but after one particularly fine coast Little Georgie ended up in the midst of the Gray Squirrel and all his family. They were scampering about in a state of great upsetment. There seemed to be nuts everywhere, little nuts and big nuts, sliding and rolling about on the ice, piled against the stone wall, hidden under fallen branches. Nearby lay the great hollow branch where they had lived. Quite evidently it had been torn from the tree by the ice storm, leaving their little home wide open to the weather and spilling squirrels and nuts all over the place.

"Luckily," the Squirrel said sadly, "none of us was hurt, but it was a terrible experience. And just look at our winter's food, scattered to the four winds!" He raced off and gathered up a few nuts, dropped them and gathered some more, which he also dropped.

"And us without a place to lay our heads," his wife wailed, "and a hard winter coming and the Folks going away and everything."

Little Georgie went back to the burrow and returned with two small baskets. "If you'd put your nuts in these," he suggested, "instead of just picking them up and dropping them again, it would help. And I'm sure some of your relations will take you in—especially if you bring your own nuts."

"I suppose they will," the Squirrel sighed, "but it's a hard thing to lose the home you were born in and your father before you, and there's all these nuts I've buried somewhere, only they're under the ice now and I doubt if I could remember where they are even if I *could* get at them. But thank you for the baskets, Little Georgie, and tell your Uncle Analdas that I guess he's right about its being a hard winter. We'll return the baskets as soon as we get settled—if I can remember to."

Little Georgie left the Squirrels scrambling and chittering over their nut supply and was starting up the Hill for another coast when he was hailed by Willie Fieldmouse. Willie had managed to tunnel up to the surface and was perched in a small shrub, enjoying the thin sunshine.

"I guess your Uncle Analdas was right about a tough winter, Georgie," Willie said. "For the Squirrels, anyway."

"Oh, I don't know," Little Georgie replied. "Those Squirrels are always in some sort of trouble. It's getting warmer already, and first thing you know this crust will melt and everybody'll be out again."

"I hope so," Willie said. "It's sort of lonesome with no one about."

Their conversation was interrupted by the sound of voices from up near the House. A moment later the Folks' station wagon came slowly crunching and grinding down the icy driveway. It was well laden with bags, among which sat Sulphronia swathed in shawls. Beside her in a blanket-draped wicker basket Mr. Muldoon distastefully surveyed the landscape. He looked none the worse for his night in the snow. Tim McGrath, who had come early to help with the loading, waved from the turnaround.

Seeing Little Georgie, the Man applied the brakes, raised his hat, and called, "Good morning, sir, and good luck to

you." Then the motor roared again and suddenly the car was far down the Black Road.

Willie and Little Georgie were all alone in the ice-covered landscape. They both had a momentary sinking feeling.

"Well, I guess I'd better tell Father and Mother," Little Georgie said thoughtfully and hopped off toward the burrow.

"This ice storm was most inopportune." Father sighed. "I had hoped that all of us Animals could be out to bid our kind friends farewell, but as fate would have it Little Georgie and William Fieldmouse were the only ones to witness their departure. Ah well, they are now doubtless happily speeding toward the Bluegrass. I wish — "

"Never mind what you wish and never mind the Bluegrass," Uncle Analdas interrupted. "Has that there Caretaker come yet, Georgie?"

Little Georgie guessed not; he hadn't seen anything of him.

"It's him *I* want to get a look at," Uncle Analdas went on. "He's what's important, him and his old woman. Better keep

your eyes peeled, you two, and see kin you size him up when he gets here." He hopped out and took up a post by the turnaround.

Little Georgie had been right about the weather — it was getting decidedly warmer. The ice crust was softening rapidly, large pools of water were appearing here and there on its surface. The tracks of the Folks' station wagon became little brooks running down the driveway.

Tim McGrath worked steadily, clearing up the broken branches and chopping them into firewood. About noon it began to rain, and he took refuge in the toolhouse. Many of the Little Animals were now able to break out, but after one look at the general slop most of them returned to their burrows.

Uncle Analdas, however, never stirred from his watching post. The Red Fox, daintly picking his way through the puddles and slush, stopped a moment to chat.

"Has that Caretaker come yet?" he asked.

"No," Uncle Analdas replied. "Held up by the storm likely. That's why I'm a settin' here. Size 'em up. Better stay around and see for yourself."

"Can't much tell by their looks what sort of garbidge Folks'll set out," Foxy said. "But I hope they'll come along soon. I've eaten nothing lately but an old Crow, tougher'n shoeleather. Got me a real elegant turkey carcass Thanksgiving, but somebody made away with most of the meat off it while I was asleep. Don't know who it could've been. Only ones could've got at it was the Fieldmice, and they don't eat meat. Queer thing."

The Fox stayed around a while but finally got tired of waiting and went back up the Hill to his den. Father and Little Georgie also came up for a short time, but they were not especially welcome. Uncle Analdas, his eyes fixed on the drive, did not care to be distracted by unnecessary conversation. So they gladly returned to the burrow and sought to quiet Mother, who was having a good worry about the old gentleman being out in the rain for so long.

So the long dreary afternoon passed, the quiet broken only by the drip of the rain and the soggy cracking of the ice crust. Father dozed in his chair, dreaming, no doubt, of the Bluegrass Region.

The quiet was suddenly shattered by the rushing entrance of Uncle Analdas. He was soaking wet, his ears were cocked at wild angles, his breath came in heavy gasps. There was a large patch of fur missing from his left hip. He was trembling with rage and excitement, chiefly rage.

"Why, Analdas," Mother cried, "whatever's the matter?"

"*Matter?*" the old Rabbit stormed when he had caught his breath. "Plenty's the matter — plenty. They've come, that's what, that there Caretaker and his old woman, and

[45]

they've got a *Dog!* The meanest, orneriest, dingblasted cur in seven counties! That's what. Almost got me, he did, the blasted, bellerin', unmannerly brute!"

"A Dog? Here on the Hill?" Mother mourned. "Oh, how terrible! With so many young ones and them with no experience and the Folks gone and the Cat gone and no one to protect us what will we ever do and it isn't as though they were used to Dogs but lots of the Animals here have never seen a Dog let alone a mean one — what kind of a Dog is it, Analdas?"

"Kind?" the old gentleman raged. "I've already told you. Mean — that's what. Poison mean, and ornery."

"I believe Mother is referring to its breed, Analdas," Father put in. "What breed of Dog is it?"

"Breed, *breed?*" Uncle Analdas snorted. He shook the rain out of his ears and stroked his bald hip. "He's got no breed, fur's I kin see. Part police dog, part terrier, mebbe part hound. Mostly brimstone and hellfire. A City Dog, that's what he is. Got no nose, no sense, no manners. Wouldn't know a Fieldmouse from a Porkypine. Just goes a-roarin' and a-rammin' into everything. Comes a-rampagin' out o' their car 'fore it had even stopped and almost had me. I run him down the field and into a mess of briars, and he didn't even know what *they* was. He knows now, but 'twon't learn him nothing."

"What about his Folks, the Caretaker and his wife and all?" Mother asked anxiously. "What did they look like?"

"How'd I know?" Uncle Analdas snapped. "I was busy. Only thing I know is, anyone'd keep a brute like that ain't got the brains of a potato beetle."

"I think," said Father, "that Little Georgie and I had best spread word among our friends of this newly arrived menace."

"You'd better," grumbled the old Rabbit, preparing for bed. "This here Hill ain't goin' to be safe fer *nobody*. Got a good notion to go back home up Danbury way. Would too, if the weather wasn't so dingblasted mean."

Father and Little Georgie paused outside the burrow to smell, look, and listen carefully, but except for the drip and trickle of water the Hill was wrapped in quiet. The Big House seemed depressingly dark and lonesome, all the windows black except for one light in the kitchen. They were somewhat relieved to hear the dismal howling of the Dog from the garage. At least he was locked up for the night.

"Georgie, suppose you find William Fieldmouse and tell him to spread the news," Father said. "He and his friends can get around very well, unless their tunnels are flooded. I shall try to locate Foxy."

He had no trouble in doing that. The Red Fox was just returning from a fruitless inspection of the garbage can. He listened attentively while Father described the newcomer.

"If there's one thing I hate it's a City Dog," Foxy said. "Always barging into everything full tilt, and no sense at all. Twice as dangerous as a Country Dog. A Country Dog now, he knows what he's doing and you can count on it, but a City Dog don't know what he's doing and nobody else does neither, till he jumps on your back. Well, I'll tell the Buck — I'm going up that way anyhow. He thinks the world and all of that young Fawn of his. That Dog bothers *him*, he's likely to move away from the Hill. The Folks certainly wouldn't like that."

"They would not indeed," Father agreed. "Such a departure would be most upsetting to everyone." He sighed. "I am beginning to feel that there is some foundation to Analdas's prophecies of a tough winter. At least it is starting very inauspiciously."

Willie Fieldmouse was greatly upset when he heard the news. "Oh goodness, Georgie," he squeaked, "I think it's just terrible, and after everything being so nice here on the Hill! I've always heard that City Dogs just blunder around into everything and kill everything in sight. Why, they're even likely to think that we Mice are Big Game!"

"Well, at least they haven't got a City Cat!" Little Georgie laughed. "That would be even worse. Tell everyone you can, especially the Gray Squirrels. They'll probably forget it before morning though."

Little Georgie was quite thoughtful as he hopped down the Hill. He hated to look at the dark cheerless house. The howls of the locked-up Dog sent shivers down his spine. Perhaps there *was* something in what Uncle Analdas had said, although he had been talking about the weather, and the weather, so far, hadn't been too bad. It was really fairly warm tonight, not at all wintry. By morning the rain would have all this ice and slush washed away.

When he reached home the roof of the storeroom was leaking badly, and he and Father had to spend a miserable, sloppy two hours fixing that.

5. *Reign of Terror*

NEXT morning Little Georgie, to his great disappointment, was forbidden to leave the burrow until Father had investigated the new arrivals; especially the Dog. Uncle Analdas had no intention of venturing out until nightfall — he was still a bit stiff and sore from last night's experience.

While dutifully obeying orders, Little Georgie did manage to stretch himself halfway out of the burrow entrance to watch Father as he nonchalantly hopped up the Hill. Father was the most skillful Dog-handler in these parts, and one could learn a great deal by observing his methods.

Now he wandered carelessly toward the house, crossed the drive, and sat down on the edge of the turnaround to scratch his ear. Almost at once the Dog rushed out from the garage, roaring and bellowing ferociously. At the very last moment Father made a short hop to the right, and the Dog shot past him. As the Dog slid and scrambled wildly to turn around, Father leisurely scratched the other ear. Half a dozen times these frantic charges were repeated, with no result save a good deal of scratched-up driveway.

Then Father hopped up the Hill toward a large bayberry clump, with the Dog in hot pursuit. Father circled the clump once, leaped aside, and froze in the deep grass. Round and round the bush the now tiring Dog raced, like a puppy chasing his own tail. Becoming bored with this, Father set off across the field, passing close by Tim McGrath, who had been watching the exhibition with considerable amusement. As the pursuing Dog passed, Tim made a swipe at him with his rake, but missed.

Father was now making for a briar patch, the same one that Uncle Analdas had made use of the previous evening.

As he approached it he slowed his pace. With the roaring brute's breath hot on his heels, Father dived into a tiny tunnel that he and Little Georgie had constructed months before. Uncle Analdas had been quite right as to the Dog's stupidity — yesterday's experience "hadn't learned him nothing." Once again the Dog plunged headlong into the briars, and his triumphant bellow changed to yelps of pain as he struggled frantically to extricate himself from the vicious tangle.

Father emerged from the tunnel on the far side of the patch and hopped back to the burrow, while the exhausted Dog limped back to the garage.

"I do not think," Father announced, "that this newly arrived canine will prove as dangerous as we feared. Of course, he is large and powerful, but unutterably stupid and inept. While his presence here is most unwelcome, and while he may cause considerable disturbance, by exercising a proper amount of precaution we should easily be able to avoid any bodily harm. Little Georgie can handle him perfectly well. I am rather surprised, Analdas, that you allowed yourself to be taken so unaware."

"Wasn't expectin' no Dog," Uncle Analdas grunted a bit sheepishly. "Specially one a-bustin' out of a car that way."

"One must always expect the unexpected," Father pronounced, "especially in the case of this creature. He is a rusher, of course, but his chief danger lies in the fact that, being so completely inexperienced and senseless, he is likely to do things which no sane, well-brought-up Country Dog would ever contemplate. I think I had best take a turn around the Hill and tell our friends and relatives just what to expect of this brute. Little Georgie, I advise you to do the same with your friends."

"What about those Caretaker Folks?" Mother asked. "Did you get a look at them?"

"They were not in evidence," Father replied. "Being City Folks, I imagine, they are given to late rising."

"*I'll* look 'em over," said Uncle Analdas. "May give that there Dog another run too. See if he's learned anything about briars yet."

"Goodness, Georgie," Willie Fieldmouse cried when warned about the Dog, "we've had trouble already. He certainly *hasn't* much sense, because he dug up a lot of

Aunt Minnie's run a while ago, and no Country Dog would ever bother to do that. He made an awful mess of the rock garden doing it, and Mr. McGrath saw him and chased him away. It's lucky he did too, because in a few more minutes Aunt Minnie's nest would have been wrecked, and she has all her winter seed stored there. She was terribly frightened, and Mr. McGrath was real mad about the rock garden. I don't think he likes that Dog."

"Who does?" Little Georgie laughed. "What's the matter with the Gray Squirrel?" For the past hour the Gray

Squirrel, high up in his tree, had been chattering, scolding, and barking with rage.

"Oh, that Dog almost got *him* too," Willie said. "He was so mad that he started scolding, and now I guess he's forgotten what he was mad about so he just keeps on."

"Good morning, sir, and good luck to you," Father greeted the Red Fox.

"Morning," Foxy replied. "Hear you and Uncle Analdas have been trying out this new Dog. What's he like?"

Father told him in great detail.

"Humph," the Fox said. " 'Bout what you'd expect from a City Dog. Won't even be any fun to run him. Well, I won't be around here much anyway. I've got to do considerable roaming if I expect to eat."

"How have you fared in the way of garbage thus far?" Father asked.

"Garbidge? *Garbidge?*" Foxy snorted disgustedly. "All they've put out so far is beer cans and banana skins. That may be City Folks idea of garbidge, but it ain't mine. Got a good idea to move down to Fat-Man-at-the-Crossroads. He's got a couple of mean Dogs, but he certainly sets an elegant garbidge can."

Uncle Analdas's report on the Caretaker was brief and far from encouraging. "He's just like his Dog," he said. "Mean. Mean and stupid. Only difference is the Dog looks strong and healthy and he's a pasty, wizendy little thing. Out there talkin' to McGrath and shiverin' around like it was really cold. Come January or February he won't stick his nose out the door — and that's agreeable to me."

"What about his wife?" Mother asked. "Did you see her?"

"A slop."

[55]

For a few days following the sudden snow and ice storm the weather turned deceptively pleasant — cold and bracing, tingling cold at night, but delightful under the noonday sun. All the Little Animals again took to collecting food for the bad days ahead. All over the Hill, in old stumps, in stone walls, under dead branches, the Fieldmice hid their little collections of seeds. The Gray Squirrel and his family, the Red Squirrels and the Chipmunks, ran and chittered from dawn to dusk as they gathered and hid nuts. The Rabbits ate clover and bark steadily, until their figures began to resemble old Porkey's.

The garden season being well over, the Animals now felt free to invade the vegetable plot and clean up the leftovers. A row of half-frozen cabbages had appealed greatly to Father and Little Georgie, and they were now peacefully enjoying another feast.

Suddenly the peace was shattered by a crashing roar and the ground between them was torn by a blasting hail of shot. Partly through instinct, partly fright, Little Georgie made a prodigious sideways leap, ending up under a nearby shrub. Almost stupefied by the noise, he managed

to glance around and saw the Caretaker hastily taking aim
again, this time at Father. And what was wrong with
Father?

Instead of streaking up the Hill (he should have been
halfway up it by now), he was dawdling around, hopping
aimlessly less than twenty feet away. For one awful moment
Little Georgie thought he had been wounded.

At that instant, however, Father made a long soaring
leap to his left. Only a fraction of a second later there was
another shattering roar, and again the ground was torn by
a load of shot, in the exact spot where Father had been.

And now, to Little Georgie's astonishment, Father hopped leisurely back to his bush, asked if he were all right,
and together they moved down the driveway, almost

tripping Tim McGrath, who was running hurriedly up it. They paused to watch as Tim, his face purple with rage, advanced on the luckless Caretaker.

"Give me that gun!" Tim roared and, when the dazed Caretaker had handed it over, threw it in the back seat of his car. "You'll get that back in the spring when the Folks come home," he went on, "*if* you're still here, which I doubt."

"What's the ideer?" whined the Caretaker.

"The idea is you're shootin' on posted land, you're huntin' out of season, you're carryin' a gun without a permit, you haven't got a huntin' license. The idea is I'm a game warden and a sheriff's deputy. Would you be wantin' any more ideas?"

The Caretaker decided he would not and slunk back to the kitchen.

The whole Hill had been aroused by the two shots. Two shots here, where no gun had been fired in years! All the Little Animals had gathered in time to witness the Caretaker's humiliation — all, that is, except Porkey and Phewie, who were slumbering, and the Mole, who was too far underground to hear anything. Even the Red Buck was peering down with interest from the edge of the Pine Wood. They all crowded around Father and Little Georgie, congratulating them on their lucky escape.

"Luck nothing," Uncle Analdas burst out. " 'Twarn't luck

at all, 'twas smartness, that's what it was, much as I hate to admit it. I seen the whole thing, an' 'twas as smart a piece of work's I've ever seen, and I've seen some good ones, done some myself, but none good as this here." He went on to describe in detail just how Father had dawdled around to draw the fire of the enemy's second barrel, how he had leaped aside at precisely the right moment, and how, knowing the danger was past, he had returned under the Caretaker's very nose and led Little Georgie to safety.

"Thank you, thank you, Analdas," Father said modestly when the old gentleman had finished. "It was nothing really. Just a little stratagem I picked up as a youth in the Bluegrass."

"Oh, of course, of course," Uncle Analdas growled. "Anything good has to come from the Bluegrass. Well, it was smart anyhow. And at least we're shut of that there gun till spring. Goin' to be a tough enough winter without a gun blastin' off every time you try to get a mouthful to eat."

6. The Power of Phewie

TIM McGRATH, of course, didn't come on Sundays.
If he had he would certainly have noticed, and done
something about, the outrageous Dog racket going on up
near the end of the garden. It was the first thing that Little
Georgie heard on emerging from the burrow, and since it

was in the near vicinity of Porkey's hole he went up at once to investigate.

It was not only in the vicinity of Porkey's hole, it *was* Porkey's hole. As Little Georgie approached he could see the Dog's hindquarters showing above the earth. The eager brute was alternating spells of frantic digging with spells of equally frantic barking. He had dug a hole big enough to hold a calf, from which he was throwing out a perfect shower of earth and stones.

Little Georgie felt pretty sure that Porkey had waked up — surely no one could sleep through this racket. He looked around hastily, found Porkey's emergency exit, and popped down the small hole. He ran through a long narrow passageway and came to the larger living room. Porkey was awake all right — that is, as much awake as he could ever get himself in the winter — and was working valiantly.

He had stuffed half his furniture and a good part of his winter hay into the entrance hole and was now busily ramming in great quantities of earth and stones. But as fast as he did, the Dog tore away his barricade from the other side. What with poor Porkey's excess weight and his sleepiness it seemed a losing battle.

"Why don't you use your escape hole?" Little Georgie asked as he helped claw down more dirt from the walls of the room.

"Couldn't squeeze through," Porkey panted. "Not with this fat on me. 'Sides, I ain't goin' to be drove out of my

[61]

home by no city cur. I'll fight him first. See can't you distract him, Georgie."

Little Georgie raced back through the passage and out through the emergency exit. He hopped around to where the Dog was working and sought to attract his attention, without the slightest success. Stamping with rage, Little Georgie hurled every insult he could think of at the laboring brute, but the Dog never even looked up. Leaping over him, Georgie kicked at the heaving flanks as hard as he could, and for a young Rabbit he could kick very hard.

Back and forth he leaped, kicking harder each time, every claw outstretched. His kicks drew blood, and once the Dog snapped at him as he would at an annoying fly, but that was all. It was clear that the Dog had an extremely narrow one-track mind. That mind was set on getting Porkey and nothing else.

As Little Georgie paused a moment to get his breath Porkey's muffled voice came from the burrow, "Git Phewie, Georgie! Git Phewie!"

Obediently Little Georgie raced across the field to Phewie's home under the stone wall. The entrance was filled with drifted leaves. He hastily kicked them aside and entered. Phewie was sleeping soundly; it took precious minutes to shake and prod him awake.

" 'Lo, li'l Georgie," he finally yawned. " 'Smatter?"

Still shaking him, Little Georgie gasped out his account of Porkey's peril. "Please hurry, Phewie," he begged. "Please!"

Phewie was willing, but oh so sleepy! He wobbled and staggered, and Little Georgie had to guide him and prop him up as they progressed slowly across the field. The Dog was almost out of sight now; only his tail showed above ground. As they approached, Little Georgie was alarmed to see various articles of furniture and hay come flying out of the hole. Porkey's barricade must be almost gone.

Phewie, now fully waked by the cold air and bright sunshine, stood to one side as Little Georgie again tried to attract the Dog's attention. He jumped and kicked, kicked and jumped, and finally, growing bolder, took a good bite at the brute's tail, but all without effect.

At last the Dog started backing out, kicking away the earth which had piled up behind him. He was almost through the barrier now, he could feel it weakening, could smell Woodchuck just beyond it. He could afford a moment's rest.

But first he would settle with this annoying pest of a Rabbit. As he stood with heaving sides and rasping breath, his bloodshot eyes suddenly lighted on Phewie, almost under his very nose. Here was another nuisance! A black and white one, a silly little thing standing there defiantly stamping his forepaws and arching his tail. The nerve of him! He'd soon settle him!

With that the Dog made a colossal mistake, a mistake that no other Animal living would have been stupid enough even to contemplate. With a menacing snarl and gaping jaws he leaped directly at Phewie! At Phewie, *Mephitis mephitis*, the Prince of Smellers, from whose path even the Wildcat and the Mountain Lion politely step aside!

Little Georgie saw it coming and made a great leap for the escape hole. As he shot down it the charging Dog was suddenly enveloped in a fine golden mist, while a strangling, overpowering stench rose to the heavens.

For a moment there was silence. Then the air was rent by hideous screams and howls as the Dog scrambled out of

the hole and started in the general direction of home.
Blinded and maddened with pain, he scraped his head
along the ground, rolled over, pawed at his eyes, collided
with trees and boulders, and never for a moment ceased
his bellowing.

Roused by his cries, the Caretaker rushed out from the
kitchen just in time to become entangled with the Dog.
Together the two rolled down the steps, and the Caretaker's
yells were joined with the Dog's, while his wife from the
kitchen window added her shrieks to the din. All told, it
was a far cry from the Sunday morning calm which usually
wrapped the Hill.

Down in the burrow Little Georgie found Porkey somewhat winded but unharmed — and sleepy. The barricade

still held firm although a great deal of pungent odor had seeped in. Phewie strolled down the corridor, stroking his whiskers complacently.

"Thanks a lot, Phewie," Porkey said. "You sure performed noble. You too, Georgie. Both of you friends in need, all right." He looked around the disordered room and sat down on his bed, which fortunately was still undisturbed. "Everything's all right, even my bed ain't been touched. Make yourselves to home. Think I'll turn in again." He burrowed sleepily into the leaves and hay. "See you . . . on . . . February . . . second. . . ."

"Guess I'll . . . join . . . him . . ." Phewie yawned. "So . . . long . . . li'l . . . Georgie. . . ."

He curled up beside his friend, and in a moment the two were snoring steadily.

Most of the Animals had been roused by the uproar, and Little Georgie found many of them gathered at the burrow when he arrived home. They were all delighted to learn that old Porkey was safe and that the Dog had received his come-uppance.

"Hee-hee," cackled Uncle Analdas. "So the fool mongril got hisself skunked! Serves him right. Maybe learn him to keep his nose out of other people's business. Won't though — too dumb. Few days he'll be out rampagin' around same as usual. Ground'll be froze then though, so he won't do much diggin'."

"This is the first occasion within my memory that Phewie has been called upon to use his Power here on the Hill," Father said, sniffing the air. "Let us hope it will be the last."

" 'Twon't be," Uncle Analdas said. "Mark my words."

The Caretaker, unable to stand the stench in the garage, tied the Dog outside, unfortunately, near the garbage pail. Foxy, having investigated the pail and found nothing to his liking, vented his disappointment by teasing and jeering at the unfortunate beast the entire evening. All night the cold air was troubled by the Dog's mournful howls, which made sleep quite impossible for the Caretaker and his wife but were sweet music to the ears of the Little Animals.

7. Fire!

AND NOW winter had really come. Day and night the wind blew from the north, a cold dry wind that reached down into even the best-built burrows. It was eye-watering, ear-tingling weather. In the fields the dry grass rustled, seedpods rattled, the bare branches gave out a low-pitched, steady whistling.

The frost penetrated deeper and deeper into the earth. Porkey's home was now safe from any digging. The Mole went down another foot or so. Little Georgie was grateful for his extra layer of fat and his heavier winter fur.

"I smell smoke," Uncle Analdas suddenly announced one evening.

"Who doesn't?" Mother replied. "What with that old pipe of yours and the fireplace smoking from the wind and all, nobody can smell anything *but* smoke."

" 'Tain't terbaccer smoke and 'tain't log smoke," her uncle said sharply. "Georgie, go take a look outside."

Little Georgie obediently trotted down the passage to the burrow entrance and drew aside the blanket Father had hung there to keep out the wind.

It revealed a terrifying sight. Through a choking, blinding smoke the whole outdoors was an angry orange glare. A wall of flame was rolling down the Hill; bright tongues leaped from bush to bush, from tree to tree. Burning wind-blown leaves flew past to start new fires all through the grass. Little Georgie saw the Gray Squirrel and his family fleeing wildly. Foxy dashed past, his plumy tail partly singed. A family of Fieldmice, squeaking with panic, shot past him into the burrow. And over everything, drowning all other sounds, was a tearing, snapping, crackling roar, growing ever louder as the fire leaped down the Hill.

"Fire!" shrieked Little Georgie, racing back down the passage and colliding with Father and Uncle Analdas, who were now well aware of what was happening. Together the three wet down the blanket and stuffed the entrance with bundles of their precious clover, despite which a great deal of choking smoke leaked in.

Mother attempted to reassure the frantic Fieldmice as the crackling roar grew louder and louder. Now it was directly overhead. For a short while the burrow was unbearably hot, then the fire passed on.

Uncle Analdas raised a paw, and in the momentary silence that followed they could hear a loud wailing sound. "Fire injin," Uncle Analdas announced. "Late as usual."

The wailing grew louder, and they could feel the ground tremble as the village pumper rumbled up through the field, closer and closer to the burrow. Then there was a thunderous, jarring crash that seemed like the end of the world to Little Georgie. The wall bulged; bundles of clover came tumbling in from the storeroom. The motor of the pumper roared. They could hear the swish and sizzle of water, shouts and running footsteps. The drumming continued steadily, the earth vibrated, pebbles fell from the ceiling.

Uncle Analdas cautiously approached the storeroom, clawed away a few bundles of clover, and was confronted by a curving black wall that smelled rubbery. He wrathfully kicked a bundle of clover. "Dingblasted injin's sunk a wheel right into our storeroom," he raged. "Fine mess that'll make of our winter's feed! Whyn't the idjits look where they're goin'?"

The fire reached the Black Road and soon burned itself out. The throbbing roar and vibration died down. They could hear more tramping and shouting as the men gathered up their hose. Then the motor roared into new life, the huge wheel spun around, grinding their painfully gathered clover into a sodden mass, spewing it far and wide over the field.

The burrow was filled with the choking fumes of oil and overheated rubber. Finally, with a great wrench the wheel pulled itself out of the hole and the engine trundled away.

Icy air rushed in from the storeroom, now just a hole open to the stars. Mother took one look and burst into tears. The Fieldmouse family burrowed into the twigs under Uncle Analdas's bed. Little Georgie, Father, and Uncle Analdas hung some blankets over the gaping hole that had been the door to the storeroom. These kept out a bit of the wind, but not much. No one slept a great deal that night.

Next morning the South Field was a desolate sight: a tufted carpet of black charred stubble, scorched trees, burned brush. The cold north wind blew little whirling clouds of black ashes that eddied around the gray boulders and settled in the burrows. Already the scorched lower branches of the cedars and pines were turning brown. The

sky was a sullen gray, the wind bitter, and it was snowing slightly.

Louie Kernstawk, the mason, arrived to look over a piece of stone wall knocked down by the fire engine. He and Tim McGrath, both well bundled up, surveyed the dreary scene.

"How'd it start?" Louie asked.

"That idiot Caretaker," Tim answered wrathfully. "If I've told him once I've told him twenty times about throwin' his cigarettes around, but you can't teach him nothing. Now look! Eighteen young apple trees ruined, Lord knows how many cedars and pines and shrubs. A fine caretaker *he* is! Wonder he hasn't set the house afire. The Folks'd done better to leave the woodchucks in charge. Least they don't smoke."

"City guy," Louie said disgustedly. "Mean-looking dog they've got there too."

"He don't bother me none," Tim said with a sour grin. "We had a little argument when they first come and I reasoned things out with him — with a pick handle."

"Well, I'll be getting along," said Louie. "Can't do anything in this weather. Cement'd freeze on you before you got it mixed."

"Nothing much I can do here either till spring," Tim said. "Goin' to take a town job till then."

His words brought dismay to Little Georgie, who had been listening from behind the stone wall. He hadn't meant to eavesdrop — he just happened to have picked out a sheltered spot for a nap. He hastened back to the burrow with his news. He hated to bring any more unhappy tidings — enough unfortunate things seemed to have happened recently — but Father and Mother must be told.

Father and Uncle Analdas had managed to plug up the gaping hole where the storeroom had been, and Mother had gathered up what clover was still usable. There was precious little of it. The Fieldmouse family had gone home, sadly picking their way through the blackened stubble of the now totally unfamiliar field.

Of course the news of Tim McGrath's coming departure threw Mother into a spell of tears, she didn't quite know why. "Oh dear," she cried, "everything's changing so what with the Folks gone and these Caretakers and their horrid Dog and ice storms and fires and no food left and all — and now him going that's always been so nice and never bothered any of us I don't know what things are coming to or whatever we'll do —"

"Aw shucks," Uncle Analdas broke in, "don't carry on so. Him goin' don't matter none. He ain't never done nothing much fer us. Even if he *was* here he couldn't stop it snowin' ner make the weather no warmer. Them's what counts, them an' eatin', an' we ain't goin' to do too much of that."

"It is an odd thing about Mr. McGrath," Father observed. "When the Folks first arrived he was rather opposed to us Small Animals. As I recollect, he often suggested the use of traps, guns, poisons, and other unpleasant methods of eliminating us. But he has slowly developed a more kindly and tolerant attitude toward us; in fact, on several occasions has even assumed the role of our protector. Perhaps he has been influenced by the example of our generous and thoughtful Folks."

"Perhaps he has and perhaps he ain't," Uncle Analdas grumbled. "Anyhow, I don't trust him. Don't much care whether he's here er not."

Next morning a very sad and grubby-looking Willie Fieldmouse appeared at the burrow. He was smeared with black from the charred grass, his paws and fur were wet with snow, and he was sniffling unhappily.

"Oh, Georgie," he cried, "it's just terrible! All the Fieldmice are going to leave the Hill. That fire burned up every scrap of food, even most of what we had stored away.

Mother and Father and Aunt Minnie and Uncle Sleeper and Uncle Stackpole and all the rest of them talked it over, and they're all of them going this evening with all their families."

"Where to?" asked Little Georgie.

"That big field of Fat-Man-at-the-Crossroads, over across the Black Road. But *I'm* not going, Georgie. I want to stay here on the Hill with you, if your folks will let me." He began to sniffle again.

"Of course you can, Willie," Mother cried. "Goodness knows it's going to be lonesome enough around here with the Folks gone and Mr. McGrath gone and all your folks gone and all."

"We feel highly honored, William," Father said, "that you have chosen to share our humble abode. I can assure you that we —"

"What're you goin' to eat?" Uncle Analdas interrupted.

"Well, sir, I have a pretty good store of my own in the garage," Willie answered, "and a few little piles in the flower garden; that didn't get burned over. I think I can feed myself all right."

"You'll have to," Uncle Analdas said grimly.

Just after sunset they went out to watch the departure of the Fieldmice. The sky was a cold green, the wind icy. Burned bushes and weed stalks whistled and rattled and shed black ashes on the sand-dry skim of snow.

Down the Hill, over the stone wall, and across the Black Road stretched the long ragged procession of refugees, most of them burdened with small bundles containing their most precious possessions. Little Georgie was amazed at their number — he had never realized how many dozens of Fieldmouse families inhabited the Hill.

Willie recognized his own family, his uncles and aunts and cousins. But there was no waving, no calling of farewells. It was too cold, and everyone was too worried, a little shamefaced, too, at deserting the Hill.

They watched until the last straggler had climbed the wall, crossed the Black Road, and disappeared in the darkness. Then they hastened back to the warm burrow. Mother and Willie Fieldmouse were again sniffling quietly.

"If people would stop that dingblasted racket," Uncle Analdas said, clambering into his bed, "maybe a body could get a wink of sleep." He stretched out a paw holding a tiny bundle. "Here's this, Willie. Found it in the field. Somebody musta dropped it. Likely your Uncle Stackpole, he never had much sense."

The bundle contained dried apple seeds. Willie stopped his sniffling, munched a few, and then climbed contentedly up to Little Georgie's bunk. "*I'm* not going to quit," he murmured sleepily as he nestled against Little Georgie's warm furry back. "I'm going to stay here on the Hill no matter *what* happens."

8. Desertions

WILLIE FIELDMOUSE'S busy, cheery presence perked everyone up considerably. He dug a tunnel up to the garage and in half a hundred trips managed to lug his small supply of seed down to the burrow. It still bore a faint aroma from the skunked Dog, but Willie didn't mind. It was food, and food was scarce. He also discovered a few overlooked stores in the rock garden and brought those down as well. Eventually he had a fair supply buried under Little Georgie's bunk, not much, but enough to last for quite a while if he ate sparingly.

"I'll make out all right," he laughed, "even if I don't get fat on it."

In the matter of food he was far better off than the Rabbits. The few little bundles of clover that Mother had saved from the wrecked storeroom were soon gone. Father, Little Georgie, and Uncle Analdas were forced to roam farther and farther afield to secure an even passable meal. Carrying home provender for Mother through the deep snow was a task they gladly shared, but it *was* wearying.

Almost daily now some of their Rabbit friends or relatives were deserting the Hill for unburned fields where food was more plentiful. Father and Uncle Analdas urged Mother to go and stay with her daughter Hazel over on Charcoal Hill, but she wouldn't hear of it.

The Red Fox dropped in to say good-by. "Hate to leave," he said apologetically, "but I've got to go down to Fat-Man-at-the-Crossroads to eat anyway, so I might's well live down there. These here Caretakers haven't set out anything eatable since the unlucky day they came here." He sadly picked his way across the Black Road, now a deep ditch between high banks of plowed snow.

Next to go were the Gray Squirrels. " 'Tisn't so much the food question with us," the Father Squirrel said. "It's mostly that dadblasted Dog. Every time one of the young ones goes down to play in the snow, here *he* comes, ramming and rampaging around after them. They're right helpless in the deep snow, he almost got my two youngest this morning. You can't keep them shut in all the time, so we're moving out. Going down to that patch of oaks across the river."

A few days later a loud uproar broke out in the Pine Wood. As Little Georgie and Uncle Analdas hastened up the Hill to investigate, the Caretaker's Dog burst from the underbrush, making his limping way homeward. He was bleeding from a long deep cut on the foreshoulder.

They found the Deer family in a great state of excitement. The Doe and her Fawn huddled together, trembling with terror, while the Buck stamped about angrily, snorting, lowering his head, and thrusting at imaginary enemies. The pelt on his spine and shoulders bristled wrathfully. The snow was trampled and liberally spattered with bloodstains.

"This Hill is no longer safe for decent, peace-loving Animals," he snorted at Uncle Analdas. "My wife frightened senseless! My young one wantonly attacked by that ravening brute of a Dog! Had he not beat such a hasty, cowardly retreat I would have stamped him to a jelly. Much as I dislike the idea, we are leaving here at once. There is a hemlock wood up Weston way where several of our friends and relatives winter every year and Dogs are practically unknown. We will go there."

"Can't say's I blame you," Uncle Analdas agreed. "That slice you give him ought to teach any Dog to mind his own business, but it won't him. Too dumb. Be out rampagin' around meaner'n ever in a few days. Well, I told you 'twas goin' to be a tough winter. *Now* was I right?"

One by one the other Animal families deserted the Hill, some from hunger, some from fear of the Dog.

Little Georgie began to find it terribly lonesome. Father and Uncle Analdas roamed incessantly, foraging for food. Willie Fieldmouse spent all his days digging tunnels under the snow, for no good reason except that he was used to it and there was nothing else to do. Porkey and Phewie, of course, were slumbering, their burrows deeply drifted over with snow. Goodness knows where the Mole was now, somewhere deep down in the frozen ground.

At night the Big House was especially depressing, with the windows all black save for one dim light in the kitchen.

The walks were unshoveled, for the Caretakers seldom ventured forth. Their Dog sulked in the garage. And Tim McGrath was gone. Little Georgie missed him almost as much as he did the Folks.

Naturally he was tremendously thrilled when one evening, just after sunset, Tim McGrath's car came lumbering up the snow-filled driveway. Dancing with excitement, Little Georgie watched intently as Tim dismounted and floundered through the drifts to the toolhouse. Little Georgie was entranced by the delicious odor of sweet clover hay that drifted from the open door.

Tim emerged, staggering under the weight of a huge forkful of hay. He carried it up the Hill to where the statue of St. Francis, swathed in burlap and knee-deep in snow, rose grayly against the dark pines. Three forkfuls he carried up, until there was a large pile of hay spreading its sweetness on the still, crisp air.

More things were brought too, in flat wicker baskets. There was a basket of grain, another of nuts, cakes of seed-studded suet, a cake of salt. There were pungent red apples, crisp carrots, fresh lettuce leaves. Then, as a crowning touch, Tim brought from the car a generous panful of bones — chop bones, steak bones, turkey bones. All these were arranged in a neat circle around the slight depression in the snow that indicated the outline of the pool beneath.

This done, Tim closed the toolhouse door, kicked the snow from his boots, and got back in his car. In the cold silence he sat a while, watching with a half-smile as Little Georgie streaked over the blue-white snow toward the burrow. A moment later he saw the four half-starved Rabbits burst from the burrow and race up the Hill, followed by the tiny skipping shadow of Willie Fieldmouse. Then he knocked out his pipe, started the motor, and the car wallowed and rolled down the driveway.

For some time the Little Animals gorged themselves in silence. Finally Mother, with a happy sigh, called, "Georgie dear, when you've had enough, please run down to the burrow and bring the baskets. We must take some of this home." Little Georgie consented gladly; perhaps a short walk would settle his overstuffed stomach and make it easier to eat some more.

Tramping up the Hill with the empty baskets, he paused a moment to catch his breath and look around. The air was tingling cold but still, so still that he could almost hear Willie Fieldmouse cracking his seeds. Overhead the half-moon rode high; the brilliantly twinkling stars seemed almost within reach. One great star hung low in the east, glowing like an immense opal. The windows of the little houses scattered through the valley shone warmly.

Then Little Georgie noticed something that had so far escaped him. Close by each house was a tiny clump of colored lights.

"Why, goodness," he cried, "it must be Christmas Eve!"

As he hastened on there suddenly came over the snowy

hills, sweet and clear and faraway, the mellow tones of the village churchbells, pealing forth their ancient message of peace and good will.

"Merry Christmas!" he called happily as he joined the others. "Merry Christmas, Mother! Merry Christmas, Father and Uncle Analdas!"

"Merry Christmas, everybody," piped Willie Fieldmouse, up to his neck in grain.

"Merry Christmas!" came another voice, and there stood the Red Fox, his plumy tail waving happily.

A tall shadow fell across the group. "Merry Christmas!" And the Deer, the Doe, and their Fawn plunged their muzzles eagerly into the hay pile. All across the snow-drifted fields Little Georgie could see the eagerly hopping forms of Rabbits coming from every direction. A long dark ribbon of Fieldmice was approaching from the Black Road.

Uncle Analdas stopped eating for a moment and grinned sourly. "Hain't seen no engraved invitations sent out to every tramp in the countryside," he observed loudly. "Thought this here spread was fur genuwine bony-fidy residents of this Hill — them that's stuck it out."

"Hush, Analdas," Mother said hastily. "It's Christmas, and there's plenty for everyone."

The Red Fox, starting on his third chop bone, said regretfully, "Too bad Phewie isn't here. He'd certainly enjoy these here tidbits."

"Who says he ain't?" and Phewie's black and white form

emerged from the shadow of the pine. He was quite thin and a bit wobbly from sleep, but filled with good spirits. "Never missed a Christmas yet, have I?" and he selected a large steak bone.

For a long time there was no further sound save the steady grinding of teeth, small contented grunts and sighs, and the clear far off caroling of the churchbells.

"'God rest you, merry gentlemen,'" Father hummed, a bit off key. "A great favorite in the Bluegrass. 'Let nothing you dismay.' I should like to propose a toast to our kindly Folks and a hope for their safe and speedy return. Hip-hip —"

"I'm fer one fer Tim McGrath," Uncle Analdas broke in. "He ain't gone off and deserted us fer no Bluegrass. Hup-hup —"

So they all gave three cheers for the Folks and for Tim McGrath, Little Georgie's voice ringing out shriller than any.

With everyone stuffed to the limit of his capacity and all the little baskets packed, there were farewells and good wishes all around as the Animals scattered to their new homes. Mother shed a few tears and Willie Fieldmouse sniffled a bit at parting with so many friends and relatives, but both were cheered by the weight of the baskets on their arms and the thought of all the good food that remained.

"Now first thing tomorrow, Analdas," Mother planned

happily, "you and Father and Little Georgie must bring down every scrap of hay that's left it's mostly lovely clover, and goodness knows where we'll put it with the storeroom gone and all but we'll manage somehow I dare say and Willie dear you must bring down all the seed you can because there's still a lot of winter to come —"

"A most commonplace way to spend Christmas Day," Father began.

"Can't think of no better," said Uncle Analdas. "Maybe it ain't the way they do things in the Bluegrass, but you ain't in no Bluegrass now. You're in the snow — up to the ears in it."

After the others had gone into the burrow he and Little Georgie stayed outside for a few moments, just to look around. Most of the lights across the valley had gone out, but the stars glittered more brilliantly than ever. The great opal-like star in the east shed a light almost as bright as the moon's.

The village bells were silent now. The only sound was the occasional snapping of a tree branch or the booming of the river ice as it cracked under the bitter cold.

"Uncle Analdas," Little Georgie asked, "how did everyone *know* this was Christmas Eve?"

"How'd they know?" Uncle Analdas replied. "Why, shucks, Little Georgie, they just *knew*, that's all. All Animals know when it's Christmas."

9. Groundhog Day

ALL THROUGH Christmas Day, Father, Little Georgie, and Uncle Analdas toiled in the bitter cold, carrying hay down to the burrow. Mother packed it away as best she could, under beds and tables, around the walls, under chairs and on top of chairs, until there was little room to move and no place to sit down. When the last armful had been stored away Father surveyed the results with considerable satisfaction.

"Well," he said, "that was a day well spent, Analdas. Barring unforeseen calamities, this should see us through the rest of the winter."

"Rest of the winter nothin'," Uncle Analdas contradicted. "'Twon't see us through January, mark my words. Winter ain't hardly begun yet."

As though it had marked his words, winter at once set

out to prove what it could really do in the way of being tough. Storm followed storm, until the snow was deeper than even Uncle Analdas could remember. The wind blew ceaselessly from the north and east, a bitter, searching wind. Occasionally there were freezing rains that iced them in for days at a time.

During these periods Willie Fieldmouse was the only one who could circulate. By digging a tunnel over to the stone wall he was able to work his way up to the surface between the stones. But once there, there was little to see. Snow and ice, he reported, covered everything; most of the fences, walls, and shrubs had disappeared beneath the whiteness. No Animal stirred on the Hill, even the chickadees and juncos shunned the burned and foodless field. Snow was drifted over the windowsills and halfway up the front door of the Big House. The Caretakers and their Dog, as far as he could tell, never ventured out. It was desolate and depressing — *and cold!*

When the others could get out there seemed very little use going. Even in the unburned fields the deep snow covered almost everything edible. They did manage to nibble some bark, but it was hardly worth the frosted ears and icy toes that it cost. They were forced to live almost entirely on the remains of the Christmas feast, which were disappearing at an alarming rate. It began to look as though Uncle Analdas was right again and they would barely scrape through January.

Father, nibbling a very frugal dinner of clover hay, said worriedly, "February second, of course, is Groundhog Day — an occasion to which we have always looked forward with considerable interest, but never, I venture, with the absorbing suspense it will arouse this year. If Porkey emerges from his hibernation on that day and casts no shadow (an occurrence we most devoutly hope for), the winter may safely be considered as over and our troubles at an end. But should the sun unfortunately shine sufficiently to cast his shadow, we will be faced with the unhappy alternative of six weeks more of the same miserable weather that we have been subjected to ever since Thanksgiving. In that case, since our foodstuffs are rapidly approaching the vanishing point, we will be forced to take drastic steps to remedy our situation."

"If all that gas means you're countin' on Groundhawg Day to help things," Uncle Analdas said, "you might's well forgit it. This here's a tough, mean winter, an' ain't nothin' good goin' to happen on Groundhawg Day ner no other day. Even if it did, it ain't goin' to bring Tim McGrath back, ner the Folks back, till they get good an' ready. They'll be lollin' down there in that dingblasted Bluegrass till we're all starved or froze to death, all they care."

"I shall continue to maintain an optimistic attitude, Analdas," Father said stiffly, "and I do not like to hear our Folks spoken of in such disparaging terms."

"Like it or lump it, is all one to me," Uncle Analdas

answered. "It's facts." He pulled up his blanket and was soon snoring loudly.

Willie Fieldmouse snuggled up to Little Georgie's back. "Georgie," he asked, "couldn't you eat some of my seed? I've got lots of it, and I hate to see you and your folks going hungry and me getting fat. Won't you try it, Georgie?"

"No thanks, Willie, I don't like it and I haven't the teeth for it, and besides, I'd finish up your whole supply in one good meal. Don't you worry, we'll make out somehow."

After some silence Willie spoke again. "Georgie, do you suppose your Uncle Analdas is right and the sun *will* shine on Groundhog Day and the Folks'll stay down in the Blue-grass till we all s-s-starve?"

"No, I don't think so." Little Georgie yawned sleepily. "Anyway, we'll know pretty soon. Now stop sniffling and go to sleep, or you'll wake up Uncle Analdas."

"I'll try to, Georgie, but I wish there was something I could do to help."

"There is," Little Georgie said. "Go to sleep."

As January dragged along, the clover hay disappeared rapidly, although everyone ate as little as possible. They all grew thinner day by day — all, that is, except Uncle Analdas. He was always so thin and bony anyway that he couldn't very well be any thinner. They were snowed in and iced in so often and so long that Little Georgie lost all track of

time. He seldom knew whether it was Monday or Friday or night or day, and didn't much care. Willie Fieldmouse busied himself digging tunnels and keeping the others posted on the weather. His reports on this were dreadfully monotonous, the weather was always bad, the only change was when it was occasionally worse.

So Little Georgie was greatly surprised and terribly thrilled one evening when Father announced that the next day would be Groundhog Day. Even Uncle Analdas showed considerable interest, fished around under his bunk, and passed out twigs from his private supply. It was a welcome treat, since the last scrap of hay had been consumed that morning for breakfast.

In ordinary years Groundhog Day had been quite a festive occasion. All the Animals of the Hill gathered with much speculation and merriment to watch Porkey's burrow, to greet him when he emerged, to comment on his changed figure, and, of course, to observe whether or not he cast a shadow. But those were ordinary years, everyone was pretty well fed and six weeks more or less of winter made very little difference to anyone.

But this year, this tough winter, things were painfully different. There would be no gathering except the four Rabbits and Willie Fieldmouse; certainly there would be little jollity or merrymaking; Father would not be called on to make his usual speech. And the question of sun or no sun was now a grimly serious matter.

Willie and Little Georgie were too excited to sleep much that night. They chattered until Father was forced to speak to them twice, quite sharply.

Next morning Uncle Analdas, as usual, was the first to be up and about. Fortunately there had been no ice storm for several days so he was able to kick and butt a way out through the snow.

"Looks promisin'," he reported, as they hastily ate a meager breakfast of bark. "Dark and cloudy — like to snow any minute."

They easily located Porkey's burrow, just outside the rose garden wall, and settled down for the long wait. Mother and Little Georgie huddled close together, Willie Fieldmouse tucked himself away between Little Georgie's forepaws and chin, while Father and Uncle Analdas paced up and down impatiently. The sky grew steadily darker, the northeast wind damper and more penetrating — snow weather surely.

All the long morning they waited, growing more chilled each moment. Still there was no sign of Porkey.

Toward noon they were joined by the Red Fox.

"Well," Foxy cried cheerfully, "Porkey still snoozing? Looks like lucky weather for us. An Elephant couldn't make no shadow today."

"The day ain't over yet," Uncle Analdas grumbled, squinting at the sky. "Deceitful, that's what it is, mark my words. Wish that fat slug'd come out and get it settled." He continued his restless pacing.

"Do you suppose maybe your Father has the date wrong?" Willie whispered.

"No," Little Georgie answered. "Father's always right — about dates." But he began to fear that Porkey never would come out.

Suddenly the snow began to quiver and heave, then there was a still greater heaving, and the grizzled head of Old Porkey appeared above the surface. Blinking and snorting, he floundered up and out of the snow.

"Well, well," he grunted, "I guess I'm good news. No shadow, none at all. Where is everybody? Ought to be a welcoming committee."

Father began to explain at great length about the ice storm, the fire, the lack of food, the departure of the other Animals, the snows, the cold.

"You all do look thin at that," Porkey said, starting to bathe. "Real thin."

"You're no butterball yourself," snapped Uncle Analdas. He glanced anxiously at the clouds where a large light patch began to show in the north. "Say, Porkey, don't you think you'd ought to get back inside? Liable to catch a cold out here, comin' out of a warm bed that way."

But Porkey, who seemed to be enjoying the fresh air and company, showed no inclination to retire. Father too was pleased to have someone besides his own family to talk to and was making the most of it.

Uncle Analdas hopped about in a fever of impatience. "Gas, gas, gas," he muttered. He plucked Mother's elbow. "Can't you stop him?" he almost begged. "Gassin' and gassin' like he had a month of Sundays, and the sky gettin' lighter all the time. Git Porkey back in his hole somehow! Git sick, have a fit, do *something*!"

Mother tried desperately to attract Father's attention, Little Georgie tried wildly to think of some way of stopping the flow of conversation, Willie Fieldmouse chittered with excitement, but Father was in full cry now, describing winters he had known in the Bluegrass. Nothing short of a major calamity could stop him.

The calamity came.

The light patch in the sky was now directly overhead and spreading. Suddenly, as though a giant curtain had been torn apart, the clouds rolled back, clear blue sky appeared, the sun shone down brilliantly. All their shadows were etched sharply upon the blinding snow!

Porkey rubbed his eyes and blinked at the sudden glare. Father broke off his endless talk and gazed around in

astonishment. "My, my," he said, "the sun seems to have come out. How unfortunate, how very unfortunate! Analdas, have you noted — "

Uncle Analdas was fairly dancing with rage. "Noted?" he screeched. "*Have I noted!* Ain't I been tryin' to shut off your gas for the last half-hour? *Noted?* Any idjit coulda seen it comin'. An' what do you do? Gas an' gas an' gas! An' that fat-headed dirt-digger, what does he do? Nothing, that's what. He come out an' seen no shadder, didn't he? Then whyn't he go back in his hole where he belongs, an' stay there? No — you can't leave well enough alone — neither of you. *He* has to set an' set, an' *you* have to gab an' gab. *Now* look what you've gone an' done! Shadders all over the place! Six weeks more of this!"

He stamped off toward the burrow, his very ears quivering with anger and disappointment.

10. Hunger

IT WAS not a happy evening in the burrow.

Without a word Uncle Analdas passed around twigs from his fast dwindling supply to everyone, except Father. Still in outraged silence, the old Rabbit nibbled at a twig, climbed into bed, pulled up the blanket, and began to snore.

After a long uncomfortable interval Father addressed Mother. "Regrettable though it is, my dear," he said, "I fear that you simply must leave the Hill and take up temporary residence with our daughter Hazel. The food situation on Charcoal Hill must be far less desperate than ours, and I am sure you will be most welcome. I will accompany you there. We shall start in the morning, immediately after breakfast. After *your* breakfast, that is. Apparently I am to have none."

Of course Mother protested and wept and insisted that they all move to Charcoal Hill, but Father remained firm. "No, my dear," he said, "my proper place is here on the Hill. I would not dream of placing any further burden on our daughter. Analdas, Georgie, and I are perfectly capable of fending for ourselves, and William Fieldmouse, of course, is well supplied with food. My mind is made up."

Eventually Mother stopped protesting and went to bed, where she worried and wept most of the night. Willie Fieldmouse did a good deal of sniffling too. What with that and Uncle Analdas's snoring, Little Georgie didn't get much sleep.

At breakfast Uncle Analdas relented a bit and gave Father a few of his precious twigs. "Got quite a jaunt," he said shortly. "Might's well have something in your stummick even if it *ain't* bluegrass."

"I thank you, Analdas," Father said politely, accepting the peace offering. "Fortunately the weather is not too unfavorable, and we should complete our journey before nightfall. I shall spend the night there and return before dark tomorrow."

"Don't hurry none on my account," Uncle Analdas replied sourly.

Mother had packed a few things in a small basket which Father was carrying. She was weeping again as she bade the others farewell.

"Now do take care of yourselves," she cautioned, "and do

try not to get the burrow mussed up too much — men are so careless although goodness knows there's not much to muss it up with no food and no cooking and all — and Willie dear do be careful and if I see any of your folks on the way I'll give them your regards — " She was still talking as she and Father crossed the Black Road, climbed the snowbank on the far side, and started their long journey across the valley.

Little Georgie felt terribly lonely after Mother and Father left. He felt terribly hungry too, so he made his way up to the Folks' rose garden, where he found a few rose bushes that the snow hadn't quite covered. He nibbled at a twig and found it much tenderer and more nourishing than Uncle Analdas's supply.

This posed quite a problem, since in return for the Folks' kindness and generosity the Animals had agreed never to invade their gardens. He was trespassing on forbidden ground. On the other hand, he argued to himself, Tim McGrath always had to cut back the roses in the spring anyway, so he really was doing them a favor to prune the roses now. Besides, he *was* terribly hungry. Hunger won the argument easily. Little Georgie ate himself a good meal of tender twigs, cut off a few, and carried them down to the burrow for Uncle Analdas.

Uncle Analdas had no compunctions at all about invading the Folks' garden. "Why, shucks, Georgie," he exclaimed, "of course it's all right. Wish I'd thought of it myself. Didn't they go traipsin' off to the dingblasted Bluegrass and leave us to shift fer ourselves? Well, we'll shift fer ourselves. What you and me better do is gather all them twigs we kin and store 'em away 'fore your old man gits back an' starts blattin' about his Sacred Word of Honor as a Southern Gentleman an' such-like rot."

So the two spent a busy afternoon and most of the next day pruning the roses and storing away the prunings under their bunks. When all was finished, Little Georgie swept the floor neatly and tidied up everything, as Mother would want it. He felt less lonesome and depressed now, in fact quite cheerful. Uncle Analdas too had shed most of his rage and resigned himself to six more weeks of winter.

Late in the afternoon it began to snow and blow again. As darkness came on Willie Fieldmouse and Little Georgie began to worry about Father, but Uncle Analdas reassured them. "Your old man may be a bit overfond of his own voice, Georgie," he said, "but he kin take care of himself — none better. Ain't no need to worry, he'll be along soon."

Sure enough, before very long Father did stumble in, safe but well blown. His face and ears were matted with snow, his paws ice-caked. In the small basket he carried a few bunches of clover, a gift from his daughter. This he passed around, accepting some rose twigs in return. To Little Georgie's great relief he chewed them eagerly without asking where they had come from.

"The food situation on Charcoal Hill," he reported after he had eaten and dried out, "while none too good, is far superior to ours. Of course they had no fire or its accompanying calamities. Hazel's storeroom is still well stocked, and either or both of you would be welcome there should you care to go."

"I ain't no quitter," Uncle Analdas snapped.

"I'm staying too," Little Georgie said firmly.

"Splendid," said Father. "The answer I had expected. Then the three of us will fight it out together."

"The four of us," Willie Fieldmouse's hurt voice piped from the shadows. "I'm still here."

"Stout fellow, William," Father exclaimed. "Your pardon. I overlooked you momentarily. We *four* will fight it out together. '*Neither rain, nor hail, nor snow, nor dark of night shall*' — the rest of the quotation escapes me. Never mind. Here we stay."

Willie Fieldmouse and Little Georgie gave a small cheer, but Uncle Analdas was already asleep.

The storm lasted for several days, during which the small supply of rose twigs disappeared rapidly. Willie Fieldmouse made frequent trips to his vantage point atop the stone wall to report on the storm's progress. Finally even the wall was snow-covered, so he was shut in too.

When the weather finally cleared Father and Uncle Analdas managed to kick and butt and claw their way to the surface, but it was scarcely worth the effort. Practically everything edible was buried. It took hours to find enough bark and twigs to make even one poor meal. There was no chance to gather any reserve supply for the burrow. Little Georgie wondered what would happen should they be snowed in again.

Ever since Mother's departure Uncle Analdas had seemed rather peculiar; now his peculiarities grew more pronounced each day. For long hours at a time he would sit in the chimney corner sucking at his empty pipe, mumbling to himself, bursting out now and again with strange remarks and queer, pointless questions.

"How fur is it to that there Bluegrass Region?" he queried one evening.

"A great distance, Analdas, a very great distance," Father replied. "I could not say exactly in miles."

"Fur as from here to Weston?"

"A great deal farther than that."

"Fur as frum here to up Danbury way?"

"Even farther than that, I am afraid, Analdas."

The old Rabbit subsided again into his mumbling and muttering.

"Whyn't you go fetch them Folks home?" he finally burst out.

"Impossible," Father replied. "Quite impossible. Moreover, my proper place is here on the Hill."

Uncle Analdas glared at him. "If *I* had a wife and young-'uns and an old uncle starvin' to death *I'd* go fetch 'em," he snapped. Then he resumed his staring at the wall, occasionally muttering, "Impossible, impossible," or, "Proper place, proper place, proper place."

The next evening he started in again. "What direction's that there Bluegrass — south, ain't it?" he asked.

"I should say, Analdas, that it lies in a generally southern direction," Father agreed. "South and somewhat west, to be more accurate."

"This here Black Road runs southwest, don't it? If a feller follered that, wouldn't it take him there?"

"It might make a start toward that region," Father said, smiling, "but there would doubtless be many other roads and ramifications. Why do you ask?"

"Got my own reasons." Uncle Analdas giggled slyly. Then he fell to staring into the fireplace and muttering, "Ramifications, ramifications, ramifications."

And again the following evening, "How'd a feller know when he got to that dingblasted Bluegrass Region?"

Father's eyes took on the dreamy look they always had when he spoke of his home state. "First there is the grass from which the region takes its name," he began, "a delicious, thick, lush grass of a distinctly bluish-green hue."

"In the winter?" Uncle Analdas interrupted.

"Well not exactly — not in the winter," Father admitted. "It is likely to be snow-covered in winter, although the snows are far lighter and of shorter duration than here. The broad acres are enclosed by the neat white-painted fences of prosperous stock farms, the fields filled with contented cattle of every description. There is found the finest horse-flesh in the world, the most delectable food, the most beautiful ladies — "

"Never mind the horseflesh and the ladies," Uncle Analdas snapped, and again fell to staring into the fireplace. Occasionally he would mutter, "Bluish-green, bluish-green," or, "Lots of cattle, lots of cattle, lots of cattle," or "White fences, white fences, white fences."

"Don't you think your Uncle Analdas is acting awfully queer lately?" Willie whispered after they had gone to bed.

"He certainly is," Little Georgie agreed. "But I guess he's just old and tired and hungry. He'll be all right when spring comes. It can't be very long now."

"It doesn't take very long to s-s-starve either," Willie sighed.

When Little Georgie got up the next morning there was no sign of Uncle Analdas. It was bitter cold outside and snowing hard. If the old Rabbit had left any tracks they were well covered now. Hastily he woke Father and told him, but Father was not greatly disturbed.

"Analdas has always been an early riser," he said. "No doubt he has gone out to look for some breakfast. He will be back soon, never fear."

But when noon came and Uncle Analdas still had not returned, Father too became worried. He and Little Georgie went out into the storm and searched every foot of the Hill. They looked carefully in the rose garden and in all the other places that the old Rabbit usually went to for food, without discovering any trace of him. Not until evening did they give up and return, cold and weary, to the burrow. They found Willie Fieldmouse in tears, and still no Uncle Analdas.

11. The Journey of Uncle Analdas

IT WAS not snowing when Uncle Analdas left the burrow, but before he had gone far the wind rose and it snowed hard. "Don't much matter," he muttered as he made his way toward the Black Road. "Soon be gittin' to where it's warmer. Jest foller the Black Road southwest."

Following the Black Road was not too easy. During the winter the snowplows had thrown up great embankments of snow on either side of the road, and the cold and ice storms had turned these into rough miniature mountain ranges; slippery, treacherous footing. Away from the road the new snow was soft and fluffy, wearying to plow through.

Now slipping and clawing on the icy ridges, now floundering in the newly fallen snow, the old Rabbit battled through the whirling flakes. Once he slid into the road, and as he crouched in terror against the bank a car roared past, its crashing chains missing him by inches. Blinded by the thrown sand and snow, choked by fumes, he scrambled back up the icy snow bank. He was shaking now with terror and weakness.

"Need something in my stummick," he decided, looking around as best he could for something edible. Fortunately a clump of young willows afforded some shelter and breakfast. But when he had eaten, the falling snow was so blinding that it took several circlings to find the Black Road again. "Gotter stick clost to the road," he thought. "Too many dingblasted ramifications, ramifications, ramifications."

For what seemed hours he plodded and fought his way along. The wind blew the snow under his fur, his ears were numb, his feet, caked with snow and ice, lost all sense of feeling. "Must be gittin' clost," he mumbled. "Don't feel so cold now." He rounded the curve by the cemetery and stumbled on.

Suddenly he came to a halt, his old nose twitching excitedly. For a moment the air brought a distinct whiff of sweet-smelling hay. "*Bluegrass!*" he exclaimed. "Can't fool me! That there's bluegrass. Blue-green hue, blue-green hue, blue-green hue . . . "

He shook and clawed the snow from his eyes and peered around. Across the road he could make out a neatly painted white fence. Farther back the whirling snowclouds revealed the dim outlines of a small barn. "Thar she be!" he cried jubilantly. "Neat white fences, stock farms, and all."

He plunged eagerly down the bank and into the road,

[106]

forgetting all about the danger of cars. One whirled by at that moment, the wind of its passing flattening him against the bank. As he skittered crazily across the road another car roaring north slammed on its brakes, skidded against the opposite bank, straightened out, and rushed on. A flying chunk of frozen snow took him in the ribs, knocking out his wind. For a few moments he lay helpless in the perilous road, then with a despairing effort he staggered to his feet and clawed his way up the bank.

He had to rest some time, his gaunt ribs heaving, before resuming his struggles. By great good fortune the barn door was open just a crack, but an amazingly small crack was enough to admit his emaciated frame.

In the dimly lit barn the escape from the wind and blinding snow, the almost overpowering smell of hay were heavenly. He collapsed and lay a while, motionless, except for his eagerly twitching nose. Now he was able to distinguish another odor, a warm, sweet, milky odor. "Cattle," he whispered. " 'Contented cattle of every description!' " Gathering his last remaining strength, he staggered across the floor to a door that was slightly ajar, pushed through, and tumbled down a step into the cow barn. A placid old Jersey cow turned mildly inquiring eyes and gazed at him over her shoulder. Then she resumed her slow cud chewing.

It was really warm in here, the windows steamed, the whirling wind seemed faint and far distant. Uncle Analdas could feel the snow melting from his ears and fur. His

ice-caked feet lay in little puddles. He dragged himself over to a pile of hay, chewed a little of it, but was too exhausted to eat much — that could come later. What he most needed was sleep, sleep and rest.

As his eyes closed he muttered faintly, "This here Bluegrass Region sure is all it's cracked up to be. Don't blame the Folks fer comin' down here. 'Twas a long, tough trip, but . . . I've . . . made . . . it."

That evening when Tim McGrath arrived home from his town job his wife said, "Tim, there's a skinny old rabbit out in the cow barn. He must have come in to get out of the storm. Poor thing looks half-starved."

Tim got a lantern and they went to look. Uncle Analdas

opened one eye, blinked at the light, and went back to
sleep.

"Well, holy saints!" Tim exclaimed. "That's that old lop-
eared rabbit from up to the Hill. Wonder what he's doing
down here? Must have come all of half a mile."

Next morning as Father and Little Georgie prepared to
resume their search Willie Fieldmouse spoke up. "Mr. Analdas," he said, "was always asking questions about the Bluegrass Region and how far it was and how to get there. Don't
you suppose maybe he tried to go down there and fetch
the Folks back?"

"A very smart deduction, William," Father said. "The
same thought had already occurred to me. What with age
and the many upsetting events and privations of this unfortunate winter, Analdas's mind is not what it used to be.
It is quite possible that he entertained some such fantastic
notion, so our first move will be to search southward along
the Black Road."

The storm had ended during the night, and the morning,
though bitterly cold, was clear and sunny. Father and Little
Georgie were able to search both sides of the Black Road
to a point at least a mile beyond Tim McGrath's, but they
found no trace of Uncle Analdas. Father's keen eye did note
the chewed willow twigs where the old rabbit had eaten,
but they might have been chewed by any of a hundred
rabbits.

They returned to the burrow about noon, where Willie Fieldmouse reported that the Red Fox had dropped by. "I told him all about Mr. Analdas being missing," Willie said, "and he thought maybe Mr. Analdas had tried to go home up Danbury way. He said he would look up as far as Weston, and he would ask the Deer to look too."

"Well done, William," Father said approvingly. "Georgie, I must notify Mother at once," and he set off for Charcoal Hill.

Little Georgie spent the rest of the afternoon searching the Hill again. Late in the afternoon the Red Fox came to report that he had been as far as Weston, with no luck. He had given the news to the Red Buck, who had promised to search clear up Danbury way. Foxy, however, had grave doubts as to whether Uncle Analdas ever would be found.

"Snow's much deeper up that way," he said gloomily. "Doubt if he ever could have got beyond the Twin Bridges. Met some of his friends and relations up around Weston, and none of 'em's seen hide nor hair of him. Sour old boy, he was, but we'll sure miss him."

Whereupon Willie Fieldmouse began to sniffle, and Little Georgie felt very sad too.

Father did not return from Charcoal Hill until late that night. He seemed thoroughly exhausted and went to bed without a word. For Father to do anything without a word was so unusual that it alarmed Little Georgie considerably.

The next morning, however, the two set out to search the Black Road again. It was snowing and blowing hard, and they were only able to go a little way beyond Tim Mc-Grath's. Even then they had difficulty in getting home. Father seemed terribly weak, stumbling frequently. Once he fell and Little Georgie had to help him get up.

When they reached the burrow Father crawled into bed and went to sleep. He slept fitfully that night, coughing and tossing. At times he seemed hot and kicked off his blanket; at other times he shivered until the bed shook. Little Georgie was terrified; never before could he remember Father being sick, and it was clear that he was very ill indeed.

The winter thus far had been bad enough; now it became a nightmare. Little Georgie struggled through the days of snow, cold, and wind, hunting for food and bringing it to the burrow, but Father could eat little of it. During the long nights Georgie and Willie Fieldmouse sat sleepless, listening to Father's coughing and hard, labored breathing. Little

Georgie was grateful for Willie's presence, it was a great comfort, but there was little that Willie could do to help, except to clean up the burrow, which he did incessantly.

Of course Little Georgie's first thought had been to fetch Mother, but he dared not leave Father for a whole day.

The days dragged by, with Father sometimes a little worse, sometimes a little better. Little Georgie grew thinner and thinner. The Red Fox dropped by now and then. All the Animals he could find had searched for Uncle Analdas, but no one had found a trace of him.

There came an evening when Little Georgie thought he had reached the limit of his endurance. Father was worse than ever. Between coughing spells he mumbled and rambled on about his youth in the Bluegrass, about Uncle Analdas, about Mother, about Porkey. Then he would relapse into long periods of silence, his harsh breathing the only sign of life. Little Georgie was in despair.

Suddenly, after one of these silent periods, Father sat up and beckoned Willie Fieldmouse to him. "William," he said, and miraculously his voice, though weak, sounded quite normal, "would you be so kind as to go up and observe the weather? If my reckoning is not faulty it will be exactly six weeks tomorrow since Porkey saw his shadow."

Little Georgie sat sunk in hopeless misery. Why bother to think about the weather? He knew what Willie's report would be. Hadn't he heard the same thing every day for months?

Then, before it seemed Willie could have had time to reach the surface, Little Georgie was transfixed by a wild squeaking and the rush of pattering footsteps. "Georgie! Georgie!" Willie squealed, bursting from his tunnel. *"It's raining!* It's not sleet or snow, Georgie, it's rain. It's *warm* rain! And the wind's from the south, and it's warm wind, Georgie, *warm!"* He was weeping and laughing with relief and joy.

Little Georgie still sat, dumb and uncomprehending.

Father smiled weakly for the first time since he had left Mother at Charcoal Hill. "Thank you, William," he said, and his voice was still natural. He pulled up the blanket, gave a deep sigh, and settled into a quiet sleep.

Still not able to believe it, Little Georgie went to the burrow entrance to look around; he had not been outside for two days. The soft warm rain was falling steadily. There was a sound of running water everywhere—rushing little brooks in the driveway, rivulets dripping from the trees and stone walls, smothered gurglings from the field itself. From the river there came small thunders, rumbling up and down the stream as the ice began to crack and stir.

The soft south breeze bathed him, enfolded him in its warmth, soaked into his thin and weary body like a healing lotion. He breathed in deeply, until he became dizzy and there were little flashes of light before his eyes.

"O-o-o-o-h, it *smells* so good," he sighed.

Willie Fieldmouse slipped a tiny paw into his. "Do you know what your Uncle Analdas would say if he was here?"

Willie asked, a bit shakily. *"Deceitful, that's what it is, plain deceitful. Don't trust it none."*

Then, after a pause, "Why Georgie, you're sniffling too."

Porkey stirred uneasily in his sleep, kicked off some of his blanketing hay, and sat up. He felt hot, the burrow seemed stuffy. He became aware of the steady drumming of rain, the gurgling of water. A slight trickle was running down the wall. The snow that covered the entrance was bulging down, dripping wetly. He inhaled a deep breath of air that seemed to reach down to his very toes.

"Ho-hum," he grunted. "Get me a stummick full of fodder tomorrow."

With a sudden roar a great slide of ice and frozen snow cascaded from the roof of Tim McGrath's barn. Water tinkled and dripped in the tin gutters and downspouts. The old Jersey rubbed her wet nose against the streaming window and mooed restlessly. Uncle Analdas, fat and sleek—for him—stirred and stretched luxuriously in the clover hay. "Don't blame nobody none fer likin' this here Bluegrass Region," he said, and yawned. "Sal-lu-berous climate, fields full o' contented cattle, blue . . . green . . . grass . . ."

Way down below the frost level Mole raised his head and his sensitive nostrils sniffed the air. It certainly was no warmer down there, and the delicious softness of the southern breeze could not possibly have penetrated the deep maze of his subterranean runs, but a slight shiver ran through his now thin frame, his tiny stump of a tail quivered. "Tomorrer," he murmured, "tomorrer I start going up."

Locked in the garage, the Caretakers' Dog howled dismally. The Red Fox came to the edge of the Pine Wood and looked down the Hill. Great dark patches of open ground were now appearing through the rapidly vanishing snow. He sat down and, pointing his sharp muzzle to the sky, gave a sharp snapping bark, another and another. Small though they were, the barks had a carrying quality that bore them across the valley all the way to Charcoal Hill. Numerous cousins there tossed back their greeting. The yapping spread through the valley clear up Weston way. The Red Buck, recognizing it, tossed his head and stamped eagerly. "Tomorrow," he snorted. "Tomorrow."

[115]

12. They Fit the Winter Through

LITTLE Georgie was wakened by a strange light in the
burrow. At first he couldn't understand it; then slowly
it dawned on him. It was sunshine! Warm, brilliant sunshine flooding into the burrow entrance where for so many
months the banked snow and ice had let in only a thin, cold
glimmer.

Willie Fieldmouse was already up and singing at his ever-
lasting housecleaning. Father sat up in his bunk, pitifully
thin, but smiling, and not coughing. Little Georgie rushed
out into a changed world.

Except for a few soggy patches of white under the evergreens where the snow had been deepest, the earth was
completely clear, steaming under the warm sun. The winter-
long snow blanket had preserved the grass, the lawns were

quite green, penciled here and there by wandering brown lines that marked the courses of Willie's now vanished tunnels. Tiny rivulets of water ran everywhere. The ground was a soaking sponge, from the river came a steady rushing roar. The layer of steam rising from the earth whirled and eddied lazily in the gentle stir of air flowing up from the south.

Little Georgie bounded eagerly up the Hill to the rose garden, where the departed snow had laid bare any number of fresh, juicy-looking twigs. He pruned off a great armful and hastened down to the burrow with them. They had a delightful breakfast. Father, for the first time, nibbled with relish; Georgie ate ravenously; Willie Fieldmouse brought out the very last of his seeds and devoured them recklessly.

Father decided on another nap, but Willie and Little Georgie dashed out into the sun again. They couldn't seem to get enough of it. Willie skittered here and there all over the Hill, inspecting his family home, searching for overlooked stores of food, but mostly just enjoying being free to run, unhampered by smothering snow.

Little Georgie dozed in the sun, digesting his breakfast, feeling the strength flowing back to his weary limbs. He was roused by Willie wildly pulling his ear and screeching into it.

"Georgie, Georgie!" Willie shrilled. "Wake up, Georgie! They're going! The Caretakers are going, Georgie!"

Little Georgie managed to focus on the turnaround, where he beheld a heartwarming sight. The Caretakers had already packed their car; now the Dog was being led from the garage and tied in the back seat. The man closed the garage door, got into the car, and without even a backward glance rolled down the driveway.

"Good riddance!" Little Georgie cried. Willie Field-mouse, dancing with joy, made a most impolite gesture involving his right front paw and his small pointed nose. They raced down to the burrow, bearing the glad tidings to Father.

"Splendid!" Father exclaimed. "This is indeed felicitous news. Do you realize that this not only terminates the menace of that unspeakable canine, but also presages the imminent return of our Folks?"

When Father could talk like that Little Georgie was *sure* he was getting better.

They hastened outdoors again, this day was too glorious to waste a moment inside—too much was happening outside. Little Georgie galloped up to inspect Phewie's and Porkey's holes, but there was still a little wet snow in the entrance of each. Evidently the sleepy-heads had not come out yet.

Suddenly Willie Fieldmouse plucked Georgie's elbow. "O-o-o-o-h, Georgie, *look! Look!*" He was too moved to squeak or twitter or dance. He just stood, his mouth partly opened, his beady little eyes fixed on the driveway, his long whiskers quivering. *"The Folks!"* he whispered.

And so it happened that Little Georgie and Willie Field-mouse, who had been the only Animals to see the Folks depart, were the only two to witness their long-hoped-for return.

Moving very slowly, avoiding the puddles, squelching through the soft spots, the station wagon proceeded up the driveway. The Man, spying the two tiny figures, stopped the car, raised his hat, and called, "Good morning, sirs, and good luck to you."

"Goodness, the poor things look half-starved," his wife said. "Tim must set out a good meal for them."

Willie and Little Georgie still stood, dumb and unbelieving, as the car moved on up to the house. Sulphronia got out and slowly moved toward the kitchen. Mr. Muldoon stepped down, glared distastefully at the wet ground, and picked his way to the front steps, where he settled down to a thorough bath.

Little Georgie and Willie were just aware that Tim Mc-Grath's car had followed the Folks' car up the drive as they again raced for the burrow bearing this fresh good news to Father. Father was so thrilled that he leaped from his bed and hurried to the entrance to see for himself. His walk was somewhat wobbly, and he was frighteningly thin, but the warm sunshine seemed to perk him up wonderfully. The sight of the Folks stirring about and of old Mr. Muldoon placidly sunning himself was an even greater tonic.

[119]

He spoke with much of his old-time decision.

"Little Georgie," he said briskly, "you must immediately
notify Mother of this happy turn of circumstances. Should
you encounter any of the other Animals on you way, kindly
request them to spread the good tidings. William, you had
best tidy up your family's domicile in preparation for their
almost immediate return."

At once Little Georgie set out for Charcoal Hill. After
the months of confinement to the burrow, of scrambling
and floundering through ice and snow, it was glorious to
stretch his limbs—to *really* run, to soar over stone walls and
small streams and puddles, to feel the hot sun on his back,
to breathe great gulps of warm soft air.

He had crossed only two fields, however, and was just
getting warmed up when, to his great surprise, he came

face to face with Mother. She carried a small basket of food and was accompanied by Hazel.

"Why, Mother," Little Georgie gasped, "I was just coming to tell you! Father's been sick but he's better now, and the Folks are back, Mother, *the Folks are back!*"

"Yes, I know," Mother said, and almost pushed him aside in her haste to get to the Hill.

Little Georgie changed his course and made for Fat-Man-at-the-Crossroads, to notify the Fieldmice. He leaped a stone wall and almost landed in the midst of the tribe—on the move. Pushing, running, squealing excitedly, they formed a great stripe of brown that flowed over stones and hummocks and through the tall dried grass and weeds.

"The Folks are back!" Little Georgie cried.

"Yes, we know," they chorused, hastening on toward the Black Road.

Little Georgie felt a bit crestfallen. His wonderful news didn't seem to be very new. He crossed the Black Road and made for the Twin Bridges. He couldn't go clear up Weston way to notify the Deer—it was too far and he still wasn't very strong—but he might meet someone who was going that way.

As he started to cross the first bridge his attention was caught by a slight commotion on the river bank. The Red Buck, the Doe, and their Fawn had, with some difficulty, just crossed the swollen stream and were shaking themselves dry.

[121]

"Hi!" Little Georgie called. "The Folks are back!"

"Thanks," the Deer answered. "We know."

After crossing the bridges Little Georgie went on up to the oak wood where the Squirrels had wintered. As he might have expected, he found the whole tribe rushing about excitedly, preparing to depart.

"It's good to see you, Georgie," the Gray Squirrel greeted him. "It's been a terrible winter, hasn't it?"

"The Folks are back!" Little Georgie announced.

"Yes, yes. Wonderful news," the Squirrel answered. "We know—heard Foxy barking last night. Nice of you to think of us, though. We'll be up later if I can ever get things together."

There was quite a congregation at the burrow when Little Georgie arrived home. The Red Fox was there. Phewie and Porkey, both quite cadaverous, had emerged from their long sleep and come over. Father was basking in the afternoon sun, delighted to have so many friends to talk to and making the most of the opportunity.

Mother was very red-eyed and weepy over the thinness of everyone and over the loss of Uncle Analdas. But she couldn't worry over the state of the burrow—Willie Fieldmouse had kept everything as neat as a pin.

"Tim McGrath's got the Saint's statue all unwrapped and the pool filled and the stones all swept off," Foxy announced gleefully. "Reckon there'll be a whingdinger of a feast tonight, for all concerned. Come on, Phewie, let's go up and sniff around the kitchen a bit. Ain't smelt chicken frying sence last fall."

He and Phewie wandered up the Hill, kitchenward, while Porkey went to sample the lawn grass, which, although last year's, still looked quite green and juicy.

"Well, my dear," Father cried, smiling happily, "it looks as though our troubles were finally over."

"They would be," Mother mourned, "if you and Little Georgie weren't so thin and peaked-looking, and I'll never forgive myself for going to Charcoal Hill and eating like a pig and you and Little Georgie almost starving, and Willie would've too if his seed hadn't held out and you sick and all. And if only Uncle Anal - Anal - Analdas—"

"Uncle Analdas *what?*" broke in a familiar rasping voice. "And what's all the snifflin' fer?"

There in the burrow entrance stood the old gentleman himself, fat and sleek, placidly chewing a straw!

"Analdas!" Mother shieked and collapsed in her chair.

"Analdas!" shouted Father, springing up from his.

"Uncle Analdas!" Little Georgie yelped, dancing a jig.

As for Willie Fieldmouse, he just spun around in dizzying circles, twittering, "Uncle Analdas, Uncle Analdas, Uncle Analdas," until he fell on the floor and lay there, kicking his heels and still twittering.

"But, Analdas," Mother finally managed to say, "wherever have you been?"

"Ben?" The old Rabbit laughed. "Why, down to the

Bluegrass, that's where. *Somebody* had to fetch the Folks
back, didn't they, and who had the gumption to go do it but
Old Uncle Analdas? They're here, ain't they? And so am I."
He settled himself in the most comfortable chair. "An' let
me tell you somethin' else. That there Bluegrass Region's all
it's cracked up to be, every bit. Anybody starts castin' down
on the Bluegrass has got *me* to fight an' don't nobody
forgit it."

That night's feast was the most sumptuous and joyous

that anyone could remember. Every Animal who belonged on the Hill was there as well as a great many friends and relations who had just come along. The Folks came out for a while and looked on from a distance, but the night, though balmy to the Animals, was really quite damp and chilly, so they soon withdrew.

The Gray Squirrel handed Little Georgie a small basket. "Thank you, Little Georgie," he said. "I've been forgetting to remember to give this back all winter."

"Well, go on and keep forgetting it," Little Georgie laughed. "Nobody's going to have to lug food around here for a long time."

There followed a long period of munching and champing, with no word spoken. Not since Tim McGrath's Christmas feast had the Animals been treated to a banquet such as this. When at last various contented grunts, groans, and sighs indicated that all had eaten as much as they safely could, everyone settled back and waited for the customary speech by Father.

For the first time in living memory, however, Father's oratory failed him. "My heart is too full for mere words," he said simply, "too filled with joy and gratitude. With joy that the long difficult winter is past and our kindly Folks have returned. With gratitude to my brave young son and his equally stout-hearted little friend who, through storm, cold, and privation, so bravely held the Hill."

"Three cheers for them that fit the winter through—Little

Georgie and Willie Fieldmouse," Foxy shouted, and the heartfelt cheer echoed all down the Hill.

Little Georgie writhed in embarrassment, while Willie dove behind Father, twittering weakly.

Porkey loyally raised his gruff voice. "Three cheers for him that went clear down to the Bluegrass and brung back the Folks—Uncle Analdas!"

Everyone responded with an equally hearty shout.

"Shucks," the old Rabbit spoke up modestly, "'twarn't much. Three, four hundred miles maybe. Do it again any time to oblige my friends."

"Tim," said Mrs. McGrath as she finished doing the dinner dishes, "that old Rabbit went away this morning, just after you left."

"Yes, I know," he said smiling. "Saw old Lop Ear up to the Hill this evening." He filled his pipe thoughtfully. "You know, it's a funny thing about them Animals. When we got there this morning there wasn't but two in sight, a little Fieldmouse and a skinny, half-starved-lookin' young Rabbit. The Folks was real upset.

"But time I left this evening the whole Hill was crawlin' with animals. Rabbits, Squirrels, Chipmunks, Woodchucks, Fieldmice, Skunks, Raccoons, all over the place. Even saw a Fox and a couple of Deer. Wonder how they knew the Folks was back and they was goin' to be fed?"

"I wonder . . ." his wife answered.

13. Later

IT WAS some weeks later.

Uncle Analdas and his cronies lolled in the warm spring sunshine in the exact same spot where they had lolled in the warm autumn sunshine last October. Tim McGrath busied himself about the garden, whistling (of all things for an Irish Yankee) "My Old Kentucky Home."

The grass of the burned field had sprung up sooner and greener than the other fields. All traces of the ice storm's damage had been cleaned up; the trees were hiding their wounds with a brave new show of leaves. Shrubs, lawns, and gardens, protected and nourished by the winter-long blanket of snow, were more lush than usual.

The Animals too had resumed their sleek, well-fed appearance. Uncle Analdas's left ear, slightly frost-bitten, was a bit more disreputable-looking than formerly; otherwise no one showed any effects of the recent hard times.

Foxy rolled over on his back and grunted contentedly. "Well, Analdas," he called, "what kind of a winter's it going to be *this* year?"

"Dunno — can't say." The old Rabbit yawned. "What's more, I don't care. *I'm* figgerin' on spendin' the winter in the Bluegrass, I am. That's the place for a feller to be, come winter. Saluberous climate, white fences, contented cattle, rich grass of a distinkly blue-green hue, world's most dee-licious food, finest horseflesh. Figger I might take Little Georgie along. How about it, Georgie?"

Little Georgie roused from his dozing and blinked at the bright sunlight. He looked up at the sparkling blue sky dotted with cream-puff clouds. He looked down the brilliant green slope with its scattered spikes of dark cedars, at the gray stone wall where their burrow lay. Leaden skies and bitter winds, cold and snow, ice and hunger, seemed things of a long-ago past.

"Oh, I don't know, Uncle Analdas," Little Georgie laughed. "I like it pretty well here. I guess Willie and I'll just stay on the Hill and fight the winter through."